Alora Funk - The Deliverance

Alora Funk, Volume 1

Stephanie Daich

Published by Phoenix Z Publishing, 2023.

Alora Funk -The Deliverance

by Stephanie Daich

Original Copyright © 2015

Cover Design:

Amber McNemar

www.ethinkgraphics.com

Dedication:

Thanks to my kids for being my biggest fans!

Chapter 1

MAYBE THIS IS WHAT birth felt like. The abyss of nothing exploding into a room of light with strange people, smells, and sounds overloading my senses. The apprehension almost drove me to insanity, and yet, at the same time, my mind went numb. I felt nothing, yet wanted to rip my skin off from the fear that crawled through my pores and strangled my body. I experienced every emotion while being robbed of every sense. It took three days to pull out of the emotional hell entirely. Just when the Benzos did their job, a strange group gathered by my bedside. They smelt differently than the medical staff, who had been my only interactions. A toxic cloud of cologne and perfume came from the strangers, seeped into my nose, and smelt like a chemical bomb exploding around me.

At first, the perfume felt like acid melting away my lungs, but then it turned to giant wads of cotton clogging them up, and I was thrown into a violent fit of coughing.

Those strange people looked down at me in an air of superiority. As my body jerked from the intense coughing, they had no compassion, just blank stares. At least the nurses had held my hand. -but these people.

"Jane. Do you know where you are?" A lady with a large nose asked, sticking it into my face. My eyes crossed, and I tried to scoot back, but my mattress prevented me from creating space from her intrusion. She got closer and closer, and it seemed she would suck my brains out or something.

The Benzos were supposed to relax me, but the presence of these strangers had a more powerful effect than the IV drug, and my nerves felt like they would explode. The fumes continued to irritate my lungs, madly clawing up my throat and forcing me to cough in the large nose lady's face.

She jumped back. "How rude." She wiped my spittle off her face but missed the drop that dangled at the tip of her nose, like the last drop of water clinging to a faucet.

A man stepped closer to me while cautiously staying out of my mouth's line of fire. I closed my eyes.

"Jane. My name is Mr. Cox. I have been assigned your case. If you could tell us any information about what happened to you, that would be ever so helpful." I shouldn't have opened my eyes because his icy stare prickled into my skin, shooting me full of frozen daggers. Orange light traced his body. I had realized everything had coloring illuminating it, even objects. People's colors constantly changed, and that mystified me.

I would later learn the colors were auras, colorful outlines of light that displayed the mood and temperament of a person. It shocked me when I discovered that most people did not see auras. To me, they seemed as normal as hands or lips. The nursing staff tended to have auras of pink, yellow, and varying shades of blue and purple. But not that group of invasive strangers. Their colorings ranged from brown, black, red, and orange.

A lady in a tight skirt said, "The hospital had a psychologist in here and was unable to complete tests and assessments on her." The fabric stretched across her thighs and shaped every curve. The skirt looked uncomfortable, and I watched to see if she might pop out of it.

I thought of her word, psychologist. What did it mean? I had undergone so many tests since my 'awakening'. So many strange people gathered around me, poking me, prodding, asking me questions. During the hospital's tests, flashy lights and beeps bounced inside my head and caused intense pressure.

I didn't want any more tests, especially from those freaky strangers.

The lady continued. "Without understanding Jane's mental compacity, we cannot properly place her." She kept pulling her skirt down as she spoke, trying to make it longer. Perhaps she should have worn something that fit better.

Mr. Cox snuffed at her and said, "I am not so worried about all your worthless tests as I am about placing Jane into a family where she can start gaining some normality in her life. We do not know if she has ever been in a family."

"Mr. Cox, the tests come first." The skirt lady said as she sucked her pen and made loud slurping sounds. Her gray aura faded into the shadows of the room.

Mr. Cox tightened his jaw and glared at the pen in her mouth. "Linda, I know you love your psychological test. I doubt the accuracy of them in her shocked state. She looks like a scared dog in a kennel. Let's place her, then after she has had a month to adjust, you can run all the tests to your little, and let me emphasize 'little' heart's content."

Blackness overtook the gray in her aurora. "Mr. Cox, that display of unprofessionalism has no place here." Linda pulled her skirt down again.

Another man elbowed Mr. Cox.

The lady with the large nose came to my side. "Jane, can we do anything for you?"

I didn't look at the nose-lady. Couldn't they stop bothering me? When the nurses attended to me, at least they used gentle voices and a soft touch. They wore the same uniforms and never seemed disappointed in my progress. Despite my fear, I felt comfort and safety from the nurses when they weren't testing me. The group of strange people made my muscles rigid to exhaustion. I wanted nothing to do with them, so I pulled the blanket over my head.

After they left, life went back to the hospital routine. Nurses sometimes read to me or gave me a stuffed animal or a soft blanket, which made me feel warmth.

I don't know how much time passed, but one day, the nurses had me sit in a wheelchair and rolled me down the hospital halls while other nurses lined the corridor and clapped for me. A few rushed to my side and hugged me.

"Oh, Jane, you get to go to your new home today."

"That is exciting."

Faces beamed, and their bright auras flashed upon the walls, making it feel like a disco of happy colors.

I didn't understand any of it. I clung to my teddy bear, looking for it to save me from the uncertainty as a nurse pushed me to a massive glass door that opened and closed on its own. I stopped breathing when I saw Mr. Cox standing beside the opening with his orange aura. Somehow, I knew they were giving me to him. I splayed my hands on my lap and cracked my knuckles. My ratty hair fluttered in the rush of air that hit me every time the big doors opened.

"Today is your big day, Jane," he said without emotion as the nurse parked the wheelchair in front of him. I didn't move, but I wanted to. I wanted to run away from him as fast as I could. But could I run, and where would I go if I could?

Mr. Cox put his hands on his hips and sighed as his eyebrows moved downward. Did he know how I felt about him?

The nurse kneeled next to me. "Jane, this is Mr. Cox. You met him a few days ago. He is going to take you to your new home." There had to be a way to escape going with him, allowing me to live in the hospital forever.

"Not yet. Not a forever home yet," he snorted. "If I had my way, then I would. But I guess we have to run all these worthless tests on Jane. So, for now, she will stay at a crisis nursery." He opened and closed his hands. I refused to look at him as he came closer to me.

The nurse put herself in Mr. Cox's face. "Sir, Jane is right here and can hear everything you say. Maybe you want to watch your words and tones."

Mr. Cox's aura turned a deeper shade of orange, like someone mixed blood into it, and his face seemed as if a giant shadow overtook it, morphing him into a hideous monster.

"Listen, Nursey, you have your duties, and I have mine. I am pretty sure a bedpan is waiting upstairs for you to change."

The nurse went red in the face, and her violet aura turned red. She glared at Mr. Cox, then turned to me. "Let me help you into the car," she said, bringing her voice kind again. Couldn't I go home with her instead of Mr. Cox?

I took the nurse's hand, and she pulled me up with the gentleness of an angel as she draped her arm over my shoulders and guided me to the back of Mr. Cox's black car. I put my fingertips in my mouth and chewed on the nails.

"Put your seatbelt on," Mr. Cox ordered. His car smelled strange, and I felt like they were locking me into a tight box that I would never escape.

The nurse pulled the strap over my chest and buckled it at my hips. She kissed me softly on the cheek, which tickled me, and I almost laughed.

"Good luck, Jane. And if you ever need anything, you can find me here." Then she whispered, "If Mr. Scary ever hurts you, you come back and tell me." She kissed my cheek. The warmth of her kiss lingered like a heated blanket, wrapping itself around my soul. Mr. Cox snorted, and my feeling of comfort shattered. The nurse had called him Mr. Scary. I liked that. I would call Mr. Cox Mr. Scary.

Mr. Scary tapped the door. "We must leave now, and you have bed sores to scrub."

The nurse again stood tall next to Mr. Scary. "You are incredible."

"Who told you?"

"I will report you."

"And I, you." He rammed his shoulder into her, pushing her out of the way.

Please don't leave me with him.

Mr. Scary closed my door and drove away.

On one of the hospital's many tests, they had put me into this tight tunnel. The tunnel felt like it was squeezing everything out of me, and I had tried to throw my body out of it, but the straps had kept me in place. Mr. Scary's car felt the same as that tunnel. I clutched the door handle and held it until my fingers ached.

I watched the hospital disappear, and tears puddled in my eyes. I closed my eyes and pictured the safety of my hospital room. I only knew life at the hospital with kind nurses. The scariest person I had ever met carried me from all that.

People at the hospital had constantly asked me, "What do you remember before the hospital?"

I had no answers. No memories. It seemed as if life started the moment the bright light brought me to consciousness. Did Mr. Scary know anything about who I was before the hospital?

"Out of the way," Mr. Scary yelled as he weaved in and out of cars, insulting almost every vehicle we passed. The zooming of objects out of my peripheral vision made my stomach slosh and feel queasy.

Finally, we pulled into the driveway of an old house. The wood shingles looked cracked and worn. Compared to many other houses we passed, this one was a mansion. Mr. Scary turned off the car and opened my door.

"Come on, Jane," he barked when I didn't move. I kept my eyes on my lap as his words berated me. "So helpless. What are you, like a teenager, yet you respond like a two-year-old." He reached in and undid my lap belt. I tensed, having his body above mine, and scooted to the middle of the backseat. He grabbed my right arm and yanked me out of the car. I gasped as his fingers tightened around mine, dragging me across the driveway.

"You are like training a new puppy." He pulled me into the house, still yanking on my arm with such force that I thought he might pull it off me.

Ding. A bell rang as we walked in, announcing our arrival. Cool air blew into my face that smelt like a strong cleaner or something. We stood in the entryway, and I bit my nails. A couple of toddlers ran up to us. One of the boys wrapped his arm around Mr. Scary's suit pants.

Mr. Scary muttered something, then ripped the boy off and shoved him as he stumbled to his knees. "You got purple jam on me!" Mr. Scary's voice deepened as his aura matched the redness in his face.

A tall lady appeared with a baby draped over each hip. One of the babies wrapped his hands through the lady's red hair. "Can I help you," she said with a smile more like one of the nurses. I wouldn't mind if Mr. Scary left me with the lady despite the massive clump of fear that clogged my chest. I could hear shouts of laughter from another room.

"Yes, I am Mr. Cox from Child Protective Services." The toddler boy stood up and wiped his sticky hands on the side of Mr. Cox's suit coat as if purposely enacting revenge.

"For starters, you can get this thing off of me. He has now ruined my suit. I will be sending you the Dry-cleaning bill."

"Tyrone, come here," the lady said, her smile now gone. The boy screamed and turned his back to her. I could feel his scream vibrate in my head.

"This is Jane Doe. We gave you the briefing on her two days ago." Mr. Scary said in a low tone as his lips turned upward.

"Oh. I wasn't here. It must have been to Crystal. How long will Jane be with us?"

"Two weeks. The first week that she's here, our psychologist will be in to run a number of tests on her. Then, it will take us about a week to place her. I suggest you locate the file we left with Crystal. You will see Jane is a special case, and you would do well learning about it instead of standing here clueless."

The lady wrinkled her forehead and looked away as her lips turned into a frown. Her breaths came out quick and loud.

Mr. Scary put his hand on his hip. "Did you get that?"

"Yes," she said, not facing him.

"Good. If you need me, here is my business card." He dropped it on the table. "And keep your eyes out for the dry-cleaning bill." The lady looked at the card but didn't pick it up. One of the babies reached into her mouth, and the lady gently pushed his hand away, but he did it again.

As Mr. Scary left, I felt my breath escape me as my muscles relaxed. The sticky-handed toddler put his hand in mine. I kept my hand limp, unsure of what to do with it, and the toddler squeezed me tightly, making his sticky mine.

"Jane, give me a minute to put these babies down, and I will help you. My name is Deborah," the redheaded lady said. I had no idea what was happening, but as long as Mr. Cox never returned, I would be okay with it.

The dining room had four cribs in it. Deborah put each baby in individual cribs and then knelt next to me with a friendly smile. I dropped my hands by my side. Behind us, one of the babies screamed as if boiling water was scolding his skin. He threw himself around his crib, desperate for Deborah's attention, but she had a way to ignore his fit.

"I know these nurseries can seem frightening. How are you doing?" Her personal care drew me into her as if she offered me a world of protection from all the Mr. Scary's of the world. Would she become my mother?

I looked away. I hadn't spoken yet and had no desire to start.

She said, "Hmm. Do you have any luggage?"

-No answer.

"I suppose I need to read your file. Are you hungry?"

-No answer.

Deborah took my hand in her soft hand. Her warm flesh spread a feeling across me like all of time would hold us together.

"I see Tyrone got you sticky," she said. "How about we start by washing your hands, and then I will give you a tour of this place."

Deborah took me into a bathroom just off the dining room. One of the babies began crying, which set off the other baby. They both wailed. Deborah gently guided me to the sink and turned the water on. When I didn't wash my hands, she put them under the water. The warmth from the water relaxed me. As she lathered on the soap, I looked into the mirror. The light seemed brighter than at the hospital, making my skin a rosier pink. I peered into my reflection's blue eyes, then' Deborah's green eyes. It seemed odd that her golden-yellow aura that encapsulated her body didn't reflect in the mirror. She had smooth hair in a ponytail, while my scraggly blond hair went everywhere. After Deborah cleaned my hands, she gently took a brush through my hair.

"Tell me about yourself."

I didn't respond.

After a tour of the massive house, Deborah sat me at the table with a paper cup of crackers. One of the babies had fallen asleep. The other still cried for her. She picked up the crying baby and, went to a desk in the corner and sifted through it with her free hand until she found a pack of papers.

"Ah, your file. You just hang there for a minute while I read about you." Deborah fed the baby a bottle with great skill, walked around, and read the file.

I loved my time at the crisis nursery. Deborah and her husband stayed for four days. They treated all of us kids with kindness. I still didn't talk, but that didn't stop them from including me in everything. When I wanted alone time, I would go to my room. Sometimes other kids stayed with me, and at times I had it to myself. I explored the library in my room and felt a sort of freedom come over me when I realized I could read. Since I had no memories, almost all my skills came as a discovery. I read five books in the Land of Stories series about the twins Alex and Conner's adventures and wished it were me. I devoured the massive collection of National Geographics. Would I ever see such wonders in my life?

Mr. Scary returned several times with a psychologist. The psychologist attempted to run tests on me, but I didn't respond to any of them.

"I knew you would fail the tests," Mr. Scary said, looking down at me. "You are just wasting my time at this point."

I didn't mind wasting his time. It was the small amount of revenge I could dish out on him. I hated the way he treated me.

Jack and Jill were the other couple that stayed at the crisis nursery when Deborah wasn't there. And yes, their names were really Jack and Jill. At the time, I didn't understand the reference to their names, yet all the other kids got a kick out of it.

The day I left the crisis nursery, Deborah and her husband were running the nursery.

"I have come to collect Jane," Mr. Scary said moments after bursting into the front door. A wall of cold air came in and chilled my bones. Or maybe the idea that I had to leave with Mr. Scary again chilled my bones. Either way, it hated the feeling and idea.

When Deborah saw him, I saw her golden-yellow aura turn orange, matching Mr. Scary's aura.

Deborah kneeled next to me and drew me into her arms. As we hugged, both our auras turned a brilliant blue. I didn't want to go with Mr. Scary. Couldn't I live at the crisis nursery forever? I gnawed my fingernails like a beaver.

"So, I take it you found a family for Jane."

Mr. Scary grasped my arm. "What becomes of Jane is no longer your concern."

Deborah's eyes turned wet, and she gave me another hug. "Good luck." She stood up and went into another room.

The drive took longer this time. The last five minutes of it, we drove into the base of a canyon. Mountains surrounded us as if we sat at the bottom of a cereal bowl.

"This is your new town, Mantua. It is too small for me. I hope you don't go crazy living here."

We drove to the edge of a reservoir. The morning air gathered in a mist above the water. Smoke billowed out of many houses. Nothing to this point in my remembrance was this spectacular. A giddiness swirled inside me. Mr. Scary pulled next to a yellow church directly across from the water.

Is this another crisis nursery?

"Come."

I jumped out of the car this time to avoid Mr. Scary dragging me. We didn't walk in as we had at the crisis nursery. Mr. Scary knocked on the door. The chilly air left fine water droplets on my skin. Birds trilled in the background. An earthy smell filled me with comfort. Since my awakening, I hadn't spent time outside, and now nature called to me. I wanted to walk around and take it all in, not meet more people, especially a new family.

No answer.

He knocked again.

No answer.

He pounded. "These hicks. They knew I was coming. They are messing with my time." Mr. Scary hit the door again.

The door opened. A portly man in a tank top stood in the doorway. He had various stains on the white tank top, which reminded me of many of the kids who" I shared the crisis nursery with. He had unkempt hair, and the fabric on his tank top wrapped tightly around his belly.

Does he have a ball in there?

"Where's the fire?" the man asked.

"I am Mr. Cox from Child Protective Service. I have come to deliver Jane Doe to your care. Are you Mike Sanibel?"

The man scratched under his belly. "I would be." He didn't move from the doorway. He seemed standoffish as he used his body to keep us from entering. He didn't look at us but kept his gaze across the street. In all fairness, the beauty over there made a better sight than a frightened girl and Mr. Scary.

"Are you going to invite us in?"

Mike peered over his shoulder into the church, stepped aside, and waved us in.

The church turned out to be converted into a home. We walked through the reception area into a large hall with three tables and found ourselves in a living room.

"The man smells like a goat," Mr. Scary muttered under his breath.

Children ran around everywhere. There were more kids there than in the crisis nursery. Indeed, this was another crisis nursery.

Mike spun around the room with his arms in the air, presenting the space to us. "Welcome," he said. He sat on the chair, pulled up to the TV, and started playing a video game.

"Mike, seriously? We have a few things to cover before I leave the child with you." Mr. Scary's posture changed as his jaw muscles tightened.

Mike scratched his collarbone. "This is the wife's project, not mine."

"Then, by all means, let us speak with Peggy Sanibel."

"Exactly, my thoughts as well." Mike kept playing his game.

The children migrated around us, their numbers growing as they gawked at me. I wanted someone's hand to hold. I went to hug my bear but realized I had left it at the crisis nursery. Deep sadness made me want to cry. That bear was my only friend.

"Mike, you are wasting my time. Please call your wife in." Mr. Scary's eyes bulged.

Mike put the controller on his chair and went to a large bell on the wall. He clanged the bell, which caused Mr. Scary and me to jump.

The obnoxious ring drew more kids in as they crowded the living room. I pulled at my shirt. Eventually, a large lady showed up. She seemed almost as tall as Mike but wider.

"Why, you must be Jane," she said as she rushed into me. She wrapped her thick arms around my body, and I melted into her. Her brilliant blue aura swirled around me.

"Peggy, your husband has already wasted a considerable amount of my time. Let's wrap this up quickly, for I have important things to do today."

"Oh, for sure," she said, releasing me. Her warmth lingered on my skin for a couple of minutes longer. She left the smell of maple on my cheeks, and my stomach growled.

Peggy shoved her hand at Mr. Scary. He took it with a look of annoyance as his lips thinned.

"I am Peggy Sanibel, and we are so super excited to have Jane. You do not need to worry about her. You made a fantastic choice placing her with us. We are such a large and happy family. Jane will feel at home quickly. Everyone in Mantua can attest to what a wonderful family we are. Did you know that Rachel said-"

"Peggy!" Mr. Scary interrupted with a voice high and squeaky. "I need to make this as brief as possible. Please, allow me to do the talking, and you do the listening."

Peggy wrapped her arms around her chest. Her kind eyes slit into orbs of hate. I couldn't blame her. Mr. Scary did that to people.

"I need to inspect the sleeping area you have for Jane. Remember, she must have her own room."

"Oh yes, yes indeed, she has her own room." Peggy changed her tone to that of a child. She bobbed her head left and right and let out a shrill giggle.

We stood there for a few minutes when Mr. Scary burst in, "Then show it to me!"

"Oh yes, yes, of course. Her room is the first bedroom at the top of the stairs," she said, pointing up the staircase in the back of the living room. Pink light shined through a colorful window. "Don't mind the stained glassed window. A pigeon flew into it. Ha-ha, get it. Stained glass. Pigeon flew into it."

"Take me there." His words came out like a roar.

Peggy let out a hearty laugh as she stepped next to Mr. Scary. "Oh, these knees of mine. They don't like those stairs. See, Mike and I have the bedroom behind the stairs, so we don't have to climb them a hundred times daily. You won't get lost. Just head on up."

"I would like you to take me there." Mr. Scary had an edge of exasperation in his voice. He looked like he might hurt Peggy if she kept up her ways. I shook, fearful of Mr. Scary. Peggy stepped even closer to him, almost touching shoulders. As if deliberate, Peggy positioned her face next to Mr. Scary's ear and yelled, "Alashia! Alashia, where are you!" I guess she wasn't scared of him.

Mr. Scary jumped back. "Seriously?" He rubbed his ear.

"Oh, that girl. I don't know where she is." She spun around as if Alashia would suddenly appear before her.

"I can take him up." A teenager said to her.

"Yes. Dayne, this is Mr. Cock."

"Cox!"

"Yeah, whatever. Take him to see Jane's room."

We followed Dayne up the stairs and went into the open room at the top. The room didn't have the same warm feeling as my bedroom had at the crisis nursery. There were no decorations on the wall. There were no books or toys—only a small bed with a ratty blanket and a dresser across from the bed. Mr. Scary opened the closet where four shirts hung.

He looked down at me. "Lucky you. Well, I guess the room meets the minimum requirements. I don't fancy you will live in the luxury lap here."

We returned to the living room, where Mike had resumed his video game. With his attention still on the TV, he jumped up. "No, no, no, no," he squealed. "Don't die. Don't die." He swung the controller around.

Mr. Scary opened his bag and pulled a file out. "Let's sign the papers, and I will leave you to it."

"You are going to have to wait," Mike said, still focused on his game. Beeps and rings came from the TV. Colorful cartoons moved around obstacles as Mike controlled them. The video game intrigued me, and I watched it as Mr. Scary tried to conduct business. At least it distracted me from the beast who was trying to take charge of the Sanibels, but they wouldn't let him. This was the first time I saw that he didn't have control.

"Where is Peggy?"

Mike did not respond as he flared his body, playing his game.

"Teen boy," Mr. Scary said to Dayne. "Go get your mother."

Dayne must have watched how Peggy dealt with Mr. Scary, for he turned into Mr. Scary and yelled, "Mother!"

Mr. Scary jumped back. "Seriously, you people."

Peggy returned. "I hope you found the room satisfactory."

"It will do."

"Oh, good. When I told the kids that we were opening our home up to a new foster sister, the girls gladly gave up their room for Jane. You see, that is what we do. We sacrifice and share in this family. Our kids have hearts of gold. Jane will do so well here. Won't you, Jane? Yes, you will. You will never find yourself lonely here, for there is always someone to play with. And, of course, as you can see, half of the neighborhood practically lives here as well. That is because our home is so warm and friendly. Everyone wants to live here. I believe it's because..."

I don't think Mr. Scary had a shred of composure by this point. "Peggy! Mike! Sign the papers. I have places to go. I am already significantly late as the two of you so rudely waste my time."

Peggy put her hands on her voluptuous hips. "Humph," she said, then reached for the papers. She scribbled her name and presented the documents to Mike. When he didn't respond to her, she put her body between him and the TV, blocking his view of his video game.

"Great, Woman, now I died."

"Sign the papers."

Mike glared at Mr. Scary, signed his name, and then pushed Peggy aside. Peggy thrust the papers at Mr. Scary but then 'accidentally' dropped them. The sheets fanned across the floor.

"Oh, dear, me and my clumsiness. Sorry." Again, she used a childish tone.

Mr. Scary shoved the papers in his bag. "Good day, people. I will see myself out." He turned and stomped out of the room.

Peggy didn't wait until he was out of ear's shot. "Well, I'll be. I have never met a ruder man."

"Indeed," Mike said, returning to his game.

Peggy left the living room.

Lots of little kids circled me.

What am I supposed to do?

The kids bombarded me with questions. I bit my nails.

"What is your name?"

"How old are you?"

"Where do you come from?"

"What is your favorite color?"

I wished I had remembered my teddy bear. I didn't answer any questions. I kept my eyes on the back of Mike.

Eventually, the kids lost interest in me. Being alone, I went to my bedroom and sat on the rock-hard bed. The wind blew through the closed window, and the room was colder than the hospital had been.

All the uncertainty and chaos of the house entered me and weighed me down. With no books to read, I pulled the blanket over me and fell asleep.

-Ding. –Ding. –Ding.

The bell in the living room sounded. The pounding of feet from every corner of the house shook my room. I sat up and wiped the sleep from my face. I supposed I should run to the noise as well, but I didn't want to leave the safety of my room.

The noise of the bustle of activity drifted up. Then the house really shook as someone came up the stairs. My door flew open, and there stood Peggy. She rubbed her knees as she filled my doorframe.

"Dearie, it is time to eat. When you hear that bell, it usually means mealtime. You want to be quick because our kids are like little vultures devouring a dead carcass. Come on, you must be hungry. Let's go get some food." She put her hand out for me, and I took it. The plump hand swallowed mine yet brought me tremendous comfort.

"You are going to love my cooking. If I can do anything well, it is cook. Just ask the ladies at the church. Whenever they need a compassionate meal, they call me."

We entered the room with three tables and a million kids gathered around them.

"Now, not all these kids are mine. As you can imagine, everyone wants to eat here. It is expensive to feed the whole neighborhood, but I never want to turn anyone down. When I was little, I used to go to my friend's houses, and their families would eat in front of me as if I wasn't there. Do you know how bad that hurt me? I never want to do that to anyone else."

"Can we eat now?"

"Yeah, can we eat?"

"Hold your horses. This is all new for Jane. Let her get her food first. When I say go, then you can eat."

Peggy handed me a plate. I stood there holding it.

"Well, go on, get some food."

Deborah, Jill, and the nurses had always dished up my food. All eyes bore into me, silently willing me to hurry. I didn't know what to do and rocked in my seat. Peggy took my plate.

"Okay, Jane, here we serve ourselves. I never like to do for my kids what they can do for themselves. I don't want to enable them. I will get your food this one time so you can see how it is done, but after that, you are on your own."

Peggy scooped a little bit of everything onto my plate. "Jane. What do you call a Pokémon who can't move very fast?"

"I know, Mom," a kid shouted.

"Christian, I asked Jane." Peggy handed me my plate. "Jane. What do you call a Pokémon who can't move very fast?"

"I know this. I know this!" Christian swung his arms around.

Peggy ignored him and answered her own joke. "A slow-poke! Ha, ha, ha. Get it."

"Can we eat now?

Peggy stepped away from the table. She smiled and counted off with her fingers. "One. Two. Three. Go!"

And like that, the damn broke, and the flood of bodies rushed over the table. When they cleared, the serving dishes didn't even have a crumb in them.

Peggy laughed. "You see. You have to be quick."

A kid reached over and grabbed the corn on the cob from my plate. Peggy swatted his hand with the back of her spoon. "Josh, don't take Jane's food. Her plate is off-limits for a week as she adjusts to our family-style eating. After that, all bets are off."

The kids elbowed each other and ruthlessly stole one another's food.

I guess I better appreciate my food today. Did I have what it took to fight for servings and line guard my plate?

Dinner ended quickly, and everyone ran from the table.

"Don't forget to wash your dish!" Peggy yelled. No one listened. Not even Peggy washed her own dish.

"Jane, I want you to come with me."

I followed her outside.

Chapter 2

THE EVENING SUN HOVERED above the reservoir across the street, casting gold ripples in the water. I followed Peggy to a peach shed in the back of the yard. From nowhere, a German shepherd charged at me. My knees knocked together as I ducked behind Peggy to protect me, but she did nothing. The massive dog jumped onto me. I tried to push it off, but it didn't listen.

At least it hasn't bitten me. -yet.

"Down, Athena," Peggy finally said in a sweet voice. The dog didn't listen and licked my face.

"Athena is our baby," Peggy said as her voice changed to baby-talk. "Aren't you, girl, you're our baby." She scratched Athena behind the ears, and Athena jumped off me. My body still shook from the unexpected lunge. Athena left several muddy prints on my shirt.

Peggy opened the shed door as Athena returned to me and sniffed my legs. Her nose left a trail of wetness on my skin.

"Have you ever been on a four-wheeler before?" Peggy asked.

A giant red four-wheeler sat parked in the corner of the shed next to a freezer.

Vroom. The mighty beast took life as Peggy straddled it. She backed the four-wheeler out of the shed and let it idle as she hooked up a small trailer. Heavy gasoline fumes lingered in the air above our heads. I liked the smell and inhaled deeply.

"That there is my pride and joy. -my fishing boat. Have you ever been fishing before?"

Again, I didn't answer.

Peggy patted the back of the four-wheeler. "Hop on, Lil' Dove," she said. The plastic seats crinkled beneath me. Athena jumped up and pushed her body behind me.

Peggy squealed. "Off for an adventure. Yippee!"

My body bounced around as she drove through her yard and onto the street. Dust billowed from beneath the wheels.

"You need to hold onto me, or you are going to fall-"

She spoke too late. I tumbled off the four-wheeler. Peggy quickly stopped it and scooped me up.

"Mercy, me. Are you okay?"

I didn't answer. Tiny pieces of dirt pushed into several open scrapes from the fall.

"You look fine," she said as she helped me back on the four-wheeler. The cold wind chilled me as she drove down the road. Athena hung out her tongue, not bothered by the cool air. The ramp into the reservoir wasn't far away. Soon, the three of us cruised along the water in the fishing boat. Damp air froze me. I thought about telling Peggy, but I still didn't want to use my words. Peggy took me all over the reservoir. The excitement caused a small smile to appear on my face, and at times, I forgot that my fingers were so cold they might fall off.

I love boating!

When Peggy finished showing off, she killed the engine.

"Below your feet is the fishing gear. Will you hand me a rod, please, Lil' Dove?"

I looked at the rods but didn't move.

"Okay, I guess I'll grab them," Peggy said, reaching by my feet. She pulled them out, and it pushed me toward the edge of the boat. I gasped as I grabbed the side to steady myself. "So, Lil' Dove, you don't talk much. What is your story? I can look into your eyes and see you have so much you want to tell me." Peggy tied a hook on each pole. She read me wrong. I had nothing I wanted to tell her. In fact, I wished she didn't expect me to talk. Peggy put a few other things on the line, and then she pulled out a fat worm.

"Pay attention, Jane. One day, you will have to bait your own hook." She put one end of the worm in her mouth and pulled it until it snapped in half. Brown goo squirted out.

Gross!

"Well, one day, I hope you feel safe enough to talk to me. You might not realize it now, but you are very blessed to come to our family. Here, no one feels alone. No one feels left out. We are the most comfortable family on earth. You don't have to take my word for it. Just look at all the neighborhood kids who would die to be in your situation. Even though you weren't born to us, you are just as dear to me as my own children.

"You are probably wondering how many kids I have. I get that. I doubt you can tell the difference between Sanibel kids and the neighborhood kids. Between you and me, it is easy to tell. Sanibels have exquisite genes. All the most beautiful kids are mine. I am not saying the other kids are ugly. They just don't have the beauty that we do. I know, I know, you see my size and might not appreciate my beauty, but let me tell you, Lil' Dove, back in my days, I was a looker." Peggy cast out the first line to the right of the boat and the other line to the left of the boat. She handed me a rod. Its cold surface instantly made my frozen hands even colder.

"You, Jane, are gorgeous."

I had seen myself in the mirror. I wasn't beautiful.

"People will be shocked when they learn you aren't part of our family. Oh, I said that wrong. You are one hundred percent a part of our family. You just weren't born from these loins. That reminds me. What do you call a bee that was just born?"

Did she honestly expect me to pick this moment to talk?

"A ba-bee!" Peggy laughed and laughed until tears came out of her eyes. "Oh, I am hilarious," she said.

Something tugged at my line, and my poll pulled out of my hands and dragged into the water.

"Oh, Jane. You don't let go." She reached into the water and grabbed the pole before it disappeared. She dropped the wet pole into my lap as freezing water spread onto me.

"Dang, it got away. If you feel a jerk on your line, give me your pole. It takes great skill to snag a fish."

Silence.

I enjoyed the silence for a split second, but Peggy had to break it. "I wish I had a joke about a fish that got away, but I do have some good fish jokes. I sometimes just go fishing for the halibut! That one is a classic. Or how about this one: Why did the fish blush? Because it saw the ocean's bottom. Those are good. I got more. What did Peggy say when Jane got annoyed at her fish puns? I really should scale back."

The darkness concealed her face. I liked it on the boat. It felt better than the chaos in the house. If only she would stop talking.

Despite loving the serenity of the reservoir, I froze. My teeth chattered, and I couldn't stop shaking.

"Oh, Mercy me, look at you. You don't have any meat on those bones. Here, take my jacket."

Peggy removed her flannel jacket and slipped it onto me. The jacket seemed more like a sleeping bag, and I curled up inside, enjoying Peggy's lingering warmth trapped in it. A weird smell came from the coat, but I tried to breathe through my mouth to stop smelling it.

Peggy continued, "It was so cold today. I saw a congressman put his hands in his own pockets."

Peggy finally stopped talking and stretched out in the boat, her legs pushing me against the side. Finally, all the noise stopped. The stillness wrapped me up like the flannel, providing safety and warmth.

The moon cast silver reflections on the lake. A trillion stars twinkled above. I could live on this boat.

"You should feel lucky it's still early spring. If it was summer, the bugs would eat you alive."

More silence, then Peggy said. "Jane, we have been joking and having a good time."

We?

"I want to get serious now. I want you to know we love you, and you are now a part of our family. I have eleven kids, and I will introduce them to you at some point. Our family just didn't feel complete with eleven. I knew there was one more kid out there for us. I have tried to get pregnant for years. Nina is our baby, and she is six. Eventually, I realized that these loins would not birth another child. That is when God inspired me to become a foster mother. When I saw you today, and your beauty, I knew you belonged to us. You are a blessing to our family, for you complete us. We are a blessing to you because we give you a family."

Peggy droned on.

How can I get this lady to stop talking?

⸻ ● ⸻

THE MORNING STARTED too early in the Sanibel house. The kids quarreled, and the parents yelled. I tried to drown it out when Alashia came into my room.

"Jane, get up! We have school today."

School! No. I am not ready for this.

I followed Alashia downstairs. None of the neighborhood kids were there, and the place seemed quieter, yet it didn't. The constant bickering didn't feel good and cast brown, red, and black auras on everyone.

The doorbell kept ringing as parents dropped babies and little kids off in the reception area.

"I babysit during the day. The money goes to feed the neighborhood. I don't mind. I love babies." Peggy said.

Mike walked into the living room, now wearing a T-shirt and pants. He looked a little more friendly.

"Kids, you have ten minutes until the bus comes! Chop chop. I am not driving late kids to school today."

Peggy looked at me. "Jane, are you up to this?"

I wanted to tell her no way, but again, I wasn't ready to use my words. Peggy studied me and then said, "Jane, how about we let you adjust? Take a few days to feel comfortable, and then you can start school."

A loud noise of an engine vibrated the house as the bus pulled up. It honked, and the Sanibel kids flew out of the door. The bus honked again, then pulled away. Several late kids ran down the stairs, but they missed the bus.

Mike shoved a bagel in his mouth, then moaned, "Great, just great! I told you I didn't want to take any kids to school today."

Peggy leaned into me, chuckling. "This happens every day."

"Let's go, kids," Mike hollered.

Peggy said, "The kids should start sleeping in the herb garden."

Mike turned to her and squinted his face. "What?"

"-So, they can be on thyme. Ha, ha. Get it. On thyme."

Mike rolled his eyes. "Ugh. Not funny. Kids, let's go."

Peggy turned to me. "Oh, it was funny."

The Sanibel kids cleared out, yet the place still felt crazy as toddlers ran around. Now, it felt more like the crisis nursery. Peggy placed a bunch of cereal bowls on a table, then went into the living room and put the TV on.

The babysat kids seemed to know what to do as they gathered around the table and ate breakfast. Peggy kept the babies with her in the living room, although she trapped them in an oval play yard. When they would cry, some older toddlers would pick them up and feed them. Peggy kept her eyes on the TV.

Toward the afternoon, my restless nerves couldn't take it anymore. I slipped out of the house.

I walked across the street and scaled the boulders along the reservoir. The nippy air froze me, yet the sun's rays warmed me. I picked a handful of weeds that grew out of the cracks. Bitter and sweet smells aroused my senses. Almost every rock had a spider crawling over it. I mountaineered the stones until they gave way to a dirt path. I followed the path around the water for the remainder of the day. A pleasant ambiance of birds and bugs heightened the tranquility of nature.

I explored the trees on the far end of the reservoir until the bus returned, pulling up to the house. It looked so tiny from far away. The Sanibel children must be home. I had no interest in returning to greet them, so I continued my adventure, imagining myself as Alex from The Land of Stories, exploring the Fairy Realm's forests, looking for magical objects.

As the sun set, the frosty air chased me home. When I entered the house, no one reacted to my return. The house once again burst at the seams as neighborhood children joined the Sanibels and some of the lingering kids whom Peggy 'babysat'. My stomach rumbled to the savory smell of dinner, reminding me I had missed breakfast and lunch. I looked at the table and saw the remains of dirty dinner dishes.

I think I missed dinner. A sharp pain rippled in my stomach, protesting the thought.

"You wanna play cards?" A kid said to me. He had a large head and a nose that seemed too small for his face. He wasn't stunning to look at, so I decided he wasn't a Sanibel.

I looked away.

Another boy put his arm over the neighbor kid. "Don't waste your time on her. She is dumb and mute."

That hurt. I wanted to crumble to the floor.

Too hungry and exhausted to do much, I went upstairs and fell asleep.

The following day seemed the same as the last. Alashia woke me up, and I integrated with the morning's chaos. When Peggy set out the cereal for the babysat kids, I made sure to grab a bowl. I couldn't eat it fast enough. When I noticed three abandoned cereal bowls, I finished those as well.

Once again, Peggy spent her day watching TV. She really got into what she called soap operas. Once again, the babysat kids tended themselves. She didn't watch the kids as Deborah and Jill had at the crisis nursery. One of the kids could wander across the street and drown in the reservoir, and Peggy would never know it.

Thankfully, that night, Peggy rewarded me with another fishing trip.

"Did you hear about the actor who fell through the floorboards? He was just going through a stage." Peggy watched me closely. "I am determined to crack that mask of hopelessness on your face. I have another one for you. Did you hear about the claustrophobic astronaut? He just needed a little space."

I turned away so I didn't disappoint her. Her jokes weren't funny. Peggy grabbed my hands; her warmth felt amazing as they thawed my frozen fingers.

"Jane, I want you to feel safe with me. I do not know what happened to you before the state found you. I don't know what horrific things you have been through. I promise you none of those will happen here. We love you, and we will show you what love feels like. Please, trust me. Open your heart to me."

Playing the part of the dumb/mute girl had gotten old. I wanted to join in conversations, yet I didn't. The idea of exchanging words terrified me. What if I said something stupid?

"What sits at the bottom of the sea and twitches? A nervous wreck."

It probably didn't matter if I said something stupid. Most of the words out of Peggy's mouth were ridiculous.

I gathered all the courage from the tip of my toes, swirling through my legs, chest, and mouth. "I don't know what to say," I whispered. It felt like iron bars fell from my lips. My face burned. Talking brought on a freedom yet filled me with dread.

"Mercy me! Mercy me! I knew you could talk!" Peggy clapped her hands and then pulled me in for a hug. Her soft body formed into mine, and I wanted to stay there forever. Peggy removed a strand of hair from my face.

"That's the girl. Keep talking. Tell me your story, please."

She expected a lot too quickly. I shrugged.

"What happened to you?"

"I don't know."

"You can feel safe to tell me. I won't tell anyone."

"I don't know. I don't have any memories before the hospital."

"Oh, my. Seriously?"

I shrugged.

"Hmm. That is so strange. Is it scary not to remember?"

"Yes."

"Does our family overwhelm you?'

"Very much."

"Hmm."

"Peggy," I stammered. "What do you know about my story?"

"Well, they found you drugged in the basement of a Russian couple in Bountiful. Their names were...Shoot, they were hard names. I made notes on my phone." Peggy scrolled in her phone, then said, "Their names were Vyacheslav and Nadezhda. I am sure I didn't pronounce them correctly. Do those names sound familiar to you?"

I shook my head.

"They didn't know if they were your parents or captors. Shoot, they were your captors, even if they were your parents. It so happens that a nosy neighbor discovered you. Let me see," she said as she read her phone. "That is right, the lady had been trying to reach them and decided to open their sliding backdoor and went inside..." Peggy read for a moment, then continued. "It doesn't really say why she went inside, but when she did, she found a closed-off cement room in the basement with you in a bed with a PICC line in you, dumping in lots of bags of fluid. At first, she thought the Russians were caring for a sick child..." Peggy read silently, then said, "but when she really thought about it, she knew that wasn't right. If parents are caring for a sick child, then they would have that child's room next to theirs. It wouldn't be in the farthest room of the basement.

Peggy put her phone back in her pocket. "She turned them in, and here we are. Were they your parents? Jane, what is your story?"

I shrugged. Until now, no one had told me about how I was found. Maybe if I had asked, someone might have. I closed my eyes and tried to recall the Russian couple. Nothing came. I tried to remember the cement room they found me in. –nothing. I couldn't even remember anyone driving me to the hospital. My memories started at the hospital, and it felt like my life began there. I could tell it hadn't since I seemed to understand much of how the world worked even though I couldn't remember my place in it.

When we returned to the house that night, Peggy decided to introduce the family to me. "Okay, let's start from left to right. That there is Nina, six; Alashia, twelve; Jill, seven; Christian, eleven; Hillary, thirteen; Emma, ten; Joshua, eight; Elizabeth, nine; and Dayne, fourteen. Who is missing?" Peggy asked.

"Rhett is at work, and no one ever knows where Corbon is," one of the kids replied.

"Well, there you go. This is your new family. Everyone, say hi to Jane."

"Hi!" all the kids bellowed out.

"Those kids over there are either kids I babysit or friends. Our home always has kids running in and out, and that's the way I like it."

"Are you adopting her?" a neighbor kid asked.

Peggy's eyes glistened with tears. "I hope so."

"Will you adopt me?"

Peggy ruffled the kid's hair. "If only."

I closed myself in my room as soon as I could break away. I hadn't remembered falling asleep, but way too soon, Alashia entered my room and awoke me. "Get up, Jane. Mom says you are going to school today."

Is it really morning? I gazed out the window as my mind woke up. What was school going to be like? Deborah at the crisis nursery had taught me about it, about the hundreds of kids gathered together for learning. If I were in grade school, then there would be recess, breaks, and snacks. In Brigham City, the next town, I would go to an intermediate school for sixth and seventh graders. I also learned that kids can be cruel to each other, especially when kids are awkward like me. Had I been to school? What kind of kid had I been? Why wouldn't my mind remember? I wanted to crawl out of my window, run away, and live in the trees at the reservoir. I could sneak back to the Sanibal's at night for dinner. No. There would be no dinner waiting. I could just fish and live off of that.

My stomach tightened, and a wave of dizziness came over me. I wasn't ready to be shoved into a sea of kids. Yet, life at home with Peggy and the babies didn't thrill me either.

I came downstairs, forcing myself to move. I grabbed some cereal and felt like I might puke it back up. Alashia came to me with a brush.

"You don't want to go to school looking like that," she said. She brushed through my hair. She didn't have the gentle hand of Deborah, but I still appreciated it. She put a bow in my hair.

"What are we going to do about those clothes? You have worn the same thing since you got here."

The bus pulled up.

Peggy said, "Hillary, you need to be in charge of Jane today. Take her to all your classes. Keep a close eye on her."

Hillary glared at me. "She looks homeless. I don't want her tagging along with me."

Beep. Beep. The bus signaled it was time to get on.

"Hillary, I expect you to watch out for Jane."

Hillary rolled her eyes. "Whatever," she grabbed my hand and, much like Mr. Scary, dragged me to the bus. At the steps, she let go of my hand and turned to me. "You are on your own now." There was an unpleasant tone to her voice, and I tried to dismiss it. She was my security, much like my teddy bear had been.

Dayne waited behind me. Hillary disappeared onto the bus, but I didn't follow. Dayne pushed from behind. "Go!"

I stepped onto the humid bus that smelt like stinky feet. Every seat had a kid sitting in it, and I didn't know what to do. I followed Hillary to the back of the bus and tried to sit next to her.

"Oh no, you don't sit with us. The back is for the cool kids. You belong with the geeks in the front."

The heavy smell of sweaty feet intensified, and something burned in my chest. I stood there, unsure of what to do.

"Hey, kid," the bus driver finally said. "I can't drive until you sit down. Take a seat."

I still didn't move. Dayne jumped up and gently led me into the seat behind the bus driver, sighing the whole time.

When we got to ACYI, I followed the kids off the bus. Dayne grabbed my hand and waited for Hillary to get off. Her groupies surrounded her, and they proceeded to walk past us. Dayne grabbed Hillary's hand and then transferred my hand into hers.

"Mom said you were in charge of Jane."

Hillary's neck disappeared into her shoulders as she looked at all her friends. "Stupid," She said. She yanked my arm so hard I thought she would rip it out of my body. "Come on, dummy," she growled. The front of the school seemed to spin around me, and my head pounded.

Hillary went to the foyer and gossiped with her friends. Her voice sped up when someone would inquire about me, and Hillary would answer, "She is just some vocally challenged special kid we are watching. Don't mind her."

-Ouch.

"Why does your family need another kid? You are like the biggest family in the world."

"I think Mom does it for the money. I can't wait to graduate, and then I am separating myself from my family forever!"

The bell rang, and Hillary turned to me. "Follow me," she barked. She sped-walked to class, and I had to run to keep up with her. She would like Mr. Scary; they were both hardhearted, kindred spirits. The only thing that differentiated them was their auras. Hillary's aura tended to be gray.

Hillary went to the back of the room and sat among a bunch of kids who surrounded her. That left no desk for me. The only empty chair was in the dead front of the room. I felt most eyes on me, so I ducked into the desk to hide, but how do you hide when you are in the front of the room?

The bell rang, and the teacher hadn't come in yet.

The overhead speakers came to life. "Welcome to school, students. Today will be the short schedule of classes since we have an assembly. Now, we must move to important information. We still have not caught the people who vandalized the school last week. We have the insurance report back, and it is estimated they caused $52,000 in damage. We have some evidence that just came in that suggests the vandals were actually students. Please see the office if you have any information on the vandalization of our fine school. You can tell us in secret, and there will be rewards for those who turn in information."

The teacher walked in and sat at his desk directly across from me.

"Thank you, students, and give this day your very best." The announcements ended.

The teacher looked us over. "Class, you look unrested. I assume it is from studying late into the night for the pop quiz we are going to have and not from partying."

Moans rippled through the room.

"Everyone, put your books under your desk and get out a number 2 pencil." The teacher reached around him and grabbed the stack of quizzes. When he faced the class, he noticed me. I gave him a start as he slightly jerked.

"Out of my class." He said.

Even though I knew he was talking to me, I didn't move.

He bent down to me with his face in mine. I didn't know what he ate for breakfast, but it stunk.

"What do you think you are doing, young lady?"

The smell swirled in my nose, and suddenly, I saw everything that had composed his breakfast in my mind. With perfect clarity, I knew he had eaten eggs, sausage, and toast with butter. –such a strange thought.

"Office, now!" He said to me.

I stood up, and my mind darkened. Kids snickered. I heard Hillary in the back proclaim, "Yeah, I have no idea who she is."

The burning in my chest moved up my throat, and I couldn't stop it. I saw a trash can by the door and ran to it. My breakfast of nasty cereal made its way into the world for a second appearance as I puked into the trash can.

"Ewe," was the consensus of the room.

"Take the trash can with you to the office."

I didn't pick up the trashcan, so he put it in my hand. He turned his head away and choked on the smell. "Out of my classroom!"

I wandered the halls for two thousand years until I found the office. I went in. Three ladies behind the desk looked at me.

"Wow, what is that smell?" Said a lady with the name tag Nancy.

I dropped the garbage can, and it tipped over. My gloppy breakfast sloshed onto the carpet.

I am such a putz.

"Oh dear," Nancy said, coming over to me. "Why don't you go lay down in the nurses' lounge? Who is your teacher, and do they know you are here?"

I didn't answer her. "Honey, what is your name?"

I kept my eyes on my hands.

She almost kneeled by me but then looked at the slimy puke-carpet. She moved to the other side and led me into a room with a bed. "Shantel, please clean up the mess," she called toward the door.

She helped me onto the bed.

"Honey, can you tell me your name, please?"

I said nothing.

"Are you okay?" When I said nothing, Nancy gently laid me on the bed and put a blanket over me. "Just rest. I will be right back."

Nancy's voice carried from the front office into the sick room.

"I think she is having a stroke. We should call 911."

"Slow down. Let's find out a little information about her first. I've called the nurse. At least let her make that decision."

"The girl won't talk."

"Let's see. The trashcan says, Mr. Hodgkin. Let's see what he knows." A crackling came overhead. "Hey, Mr. Hodgkin, this is Shantel in the office. You sent a sick kid to the office. Can you tell us her name and what is wrong with her?"

"I don't know who she is. She was sluffing in my class. I sent her to you, not soon enough, though. She puked in my garbage can."

"Does anyone in your class know who she is?"

"Class, who can tell me about the sluffer?"

I couldn't hear the kid who spoke, but soon, Mr. Hodgkin's voice returned. "It turns out the girl is a Sanibel. I guess a new Sanibel. Today is her first day of school."

"Do you have any other Sanibels in your class?" Nancy asked.

"Yes, Hillary."

"Please send her down."

I drifted to sleep, but Hillary and Nancy soon woke me.

"Oh, poor Jane," Hillary said, suddenly caring about my well-being. "Are you sick?" This was not The Hillary I knew. She looked like Hillary but acted like someone who cared about me.

I pulled the cover over my head.

"Hillary, we don't have any records for a new Sanibel."

"Oh, she isn't a Sanibel. Her name is Jane Doe."

"Jane Doe. That is highly unlikely. What kind of prank are you two playing?"

"No, really. That is her name. She is a foster kid."

"Does your home really need one more kid?"

"My thoughts exactly."

Nancy said, "Do you think she is having a stroke? She won't talk to us."

"Oh no, she is just dumb and mute. You know, special. Mom decided she didn't have enough on her plate being a failure of a mom, so she brought in another child to screw up their lives as well."

Nancy's voice tightened, "Hillary, that was uncalled for. You have a lovely mom."

"Whatever. Anyways, did you hear that story on the news a couple of months ago about the girl they found in Bountiful? The story about the girl they found chained in the Russian's basement. Yeah, she was guarded by three Doberman pinchers and two Rottweilers. Anyways, that girl is Jane Doe. I guess since they still don't know her name, we call her Jane Doe."

"Hillary, that sounds like a tale."

I heard Shantel enter the room. "No, it is true. I watched it on the news. I don't know if this girl here is actually the girl from the news, but it did happen."

Hillary popped her gum and said, "See, told ya."

"Well, nonetheless, if this girl belongs to your family, then we need to call your mother in. She must register her first."

Nancy said, "Hillary, you can go back to class."

"Must I?"

"Yes."

"Okay, but good luck getting my mom in."

"Why is that?"

"Because I think the house would have to be on fire to pull her away from her soaps."

———◉———

PEGGY HADN'T TALKED to me since she picked me up from school, treating me like I had done something wrong. She sped through the canyon with deep sighs, driving almost as dangerous as Mr. Scary. Her aura burned crimson red.

"I don't have time for this," she sputtered, sounding like Mr. Scary. "Today is the episode where Sandra wakes up from her coma to find out her husband has been sleeping with the nurse." Peggy hardly had the car put in park when she ran into the house. It wasn't until I got inside that I realized she had left all those little kids home alone.

Unsure of what to do, I sat on the couch and dazed off, looking at the television. Springs under the cushions bit my butt. As I gazed at the TV, something strange happened. I saw all the television parts in my mind, and then I watched them separate and could see each individual component of it, and knew their names, such as the cathode ray tubes. The logic board separated, and I saw the transformers, chokes, electric wiring, coils, and resistors.

"Hello, Mr. Cock." Peggy's voice shattered my mental image. A commercial played as she spoke on the phone. "Yes, this is Peggy Sanibel. Apparently, your department dropped the ball and didn't register Jane Doe to school. I have a list of vital paperwork that must be submitted before she can return. I will email the requirements to you. Please finalize this ASAP. I am a foster mom but not a homeschool teacher. Tah, tah."

She put the phone in her lap just as her soap opera came back on. "Perfect timing," she giggled.

The weekend came and went. The house filled with every child in the neighborhood. With the intrusion of kids came the commandeering of my room. Lots of Sanibels and neighbors moved their blankets and stuffed animals in. My room became a night party, which I hated. At least Friday and Saturday night, she rescued me from chaos for fishing. We had tremendous luck and filled the freezer in the shed with fish. I took the chance to practice speaking with Peggy. She was a different person on the boat. She seemed to care as she doted her attention to me. She still bragged nonstop about what a great mom she was. I was starting to have my doubts as I watched her spend no time or attention on her kids. The only thing she excelled at was cooking.

I had to wait until Tuesday to start school. I was more nervous than before. There was no way I wanted to go through that again.

The bus honked and, on my way, out the door. Mike stopped me.

"I am taking you to school."

Relief rushed over me. At least I wouldn't have to ride on that bus again.

"Hillary, Dayne, you wanna ride?"

From outside, Hillary poked her head into the house. "I wouldn't be caught dead seen in that shaggin' waggin."

I followed Mike outside, where he led me to a mini-bus. "The kids are embarrassed by our bus, but we were lucky. Willow Creek Assisted Living donated it to us. It needed a lot of work, but that was no big deal for me. Now our whole family can ride together."

Dayne joined us but didn't talk to me.

Once at school, I trailed behind Mike into the office. I looked at my hands, embarrassed to see the secretaries again. Nancy came to my side and hugged me.

"Hi Jane, you are looking much better." She looked up at Mike. "Hi, Mr. Sanibel. How is work at the plant?" She seemed to perk up as she spoke and giggled a lot.

Mike stood erect for the first time, and his voice bounced enthusiastically. "Good, Nancy. I haven't seen you for a minute. I hope my kids are being good to you." I also noticed the solid, musky cologne he wore. Usually, he smelt like BO. Suddenly, my mind separated the ingredients in his cologne. Bergamot, patchouli, sandalwood, sambac, white musk... *What is going on with me? Is this normal? I don't even know what those words mean. Like sambac!*

Nancy spoke, "Mike, your new foster daughter threw us for a loop. I thought she was having a stroke the last time she was here. I am glad she wasn't."

Mike put his arm over my shoulder and pulled me into him. "Poor dear," he said. He had barely known I existed up to that point. "She was rescued from the basement of Russian spies who were running terrible experiments on her body. Did you know she received daily torture? They found her tied up with barbed wire and probes in her head. It is no wonder that she has selected mutism. I don't blame her for not talking. Give her time, and you won't be able to shut her up, am I right?" He puffed his chest out and stared at Nancy with a strange expression that I hadn't seen him use before.

Nancy laughed and laughed, and Mike joined in. "The wife has done a fabulous job with her, and Jane talks to her on their nightly bonding trips at the reservoir. Jane will feel at home in no time."

He reached forward and touched Nancy's hand. Nancy's face changed to a rosy red. "Well, Jane is, um, she is, um..." Nancy suddenly seemed to have trouble speaking, "...she is, um, ready to start seventh grade. We weren't sure how old she was. The Department of Child

Services said she might be thirteen or fourteen." Nancy twirled her finger through her hair.

Mike replied, "Good enough for me."

The two laughed again. Who was this man in the office? Mike never acted like this.

"Would you like to walk her to her first class?" Nancy leaned across the counter, and her face almost touched Mike's face.

"Oh no. I learned long ago that the kids like to pretend I died. I wouldn't embarrass Jane on her first day of school like that."

Nancy laughed. "Okay, we will figure it out."

After Mike left, Nancy took me to a back office and showed me a bulletin board with student faces on it.

"These are members of our Hope Club. We know how intimidating the first few months at a new school are. These students believe in the 4 Cs- Compassion, connection, commitment, and confidence. If you are willing, we can assign you to a couple of students who will walk to your classes with you and sit with you at lunch. Can I see your schedule?"

I didn't know what she meant.

"That paper you are holding. Can I see it?" Nancy took the paper from my hand. "Okay, let's see. We try to place you with students who have the same lunch as you. Let's see. You have B lunch. Oh look, your sister Hillary also has B lunch. Let's keep it simple, and she can be your hope-buddy."

Hillary hates me! I had to react. I wasn't ready for words yet, so I vigorously shook my head.

"Oh, okay. That surprises me. Hillary is such a sweetie. Okay, let's see." She pointed to a few faces. "Rhonda, Jill, Mike, or Tim. All of them are wonderful. You won't go wrong with who you pick.

I studied Rhonda's face in the pictures, and suddenly, glimmering stars shone from the picture. Nancy didn't seem to notice, or maybe she was used to it. Did stars usually glimmer from images? I looked at

Rhonda again, knowing she had Somalian and British in her bloodline. Jill had Irish and English. Mike had Latin and Aztec. Tim had...

"Do you want me to pick for you?"

I shook my head and pointed to Rhonda. She had kinder eyes than the rest.

"Good choice."

As I waited for Rhonda, an announcement came through the crackly speakers.

"Dear students, we have had new information come in on the vandalization of the school. The police have been able to find a few fingerprints and are now evaluating. Please remember to let us know if you have any information, and we will keep your name anonymous."

"They do the announcement in the back room," Nancy said to me as if I wanted to know. When the announcements finished, Nancy called Rhonda to the office, and she appeared.

"Hey, Nancy. What's up?" Rhonda had a deep accent. Her brown skin looked silky and pure, without any blemishes.

"Rhonda, this is Jane Doe. She is a new student at the school. Do you know Hillary Sandibel? Of course, you do. This is her foster sister."

Rhonda's eyes opened wide.

"She has picked you as her hope-buddy. Can you escort her to her classes for the next few weeks? And then, of course, invite her to sit with you and your friends at lunch?"

"Of course, I can, Nancy." Rhonda turned to me and put her hand out. I didn't take it. Her eyes relaxed. Her aura burned violet. She said, "Hi, Jane. Can I see your schedule?"

Nancy still had it and handed it to Rhonda. It crinkled in Rhonda's hand as she snapped a picture of it with her phone.

"Perfect, we have 1st, 2nd, and 6th period together. That will make it easy. Jane, are you ready to go?"

I looked at her and did nothing.

Rhonda looped her arm through mine and skipped out of the office. I had to jog to keep up with her. I found myself intrigued by Rhonda's smile and the sweet smell of tangerine on her. Perhaps she would be my new security.

"Jane, I heard about you. You are that girl they found wrapped in chains in the trunk of the Russian's car. That must have been scary for you. Wow, you are like a celebrity. So, what was it like being a prisoner like that?"

I didn't answer.

"I heard you are mute and... No, let me say it better. Hmmm. Let me think. I heard you don't talk. Do you understand me? Maybe you don't speak English. I bet that is what it is. We are all trying to talk to you, and you are Russian." Her hands moved around as she spoke—such animation.

She stopped at a classroom. "Well, this is it. This is Mrs. Jennings. She is awesome. You will love her. She makes science fun."

We entered the classroom, and all eyes were on me. I looked at my hands.

"Mrs. Jennings, this is Jane Doe. She is Russian, so she might not understand you. But anyway, where would you like her to sit?"

"How about you pull a chair up to your table, and she can be lab partners with you and George. Welcome, Jane."

Rhonda still had my arm and guided me to a table with George. He had deep auburn hair and smelt of Doritos.

"Jane, we were just going over Adenosine triphosphate, also known as ATP, which is a molecule that carries energy within cells. All living things use ATP. In addition to being used as an energy source, it is also used in signal transduction pathways for cell communication."

In my mind, I saw the chemical makeup of ATP, with its molecule of adenosine and three phosphate groups. I knew that ATP was the primary energy carrier in all cellular activity.

How do I know this?

Chapter 3

THE LONG SCHOOL DAY overwhelmed me, and finally, I could relax on the fishing boat. The night air seemed colder than usual. I wrapped a blanket tightly over my shoulders and imagined the breeze carrying away all my anxiety.

"How was school?" Peggy asked as she cast her line to the left of the boat. She picked up my rod and handed it to me. "You need to set up your own line from now on." She dropped the tackle box into my lap. I had watched her enough and pulled the hook, spinner, and weights out.

"So, how was school?"

"Scary."

"And?"

"They put me with a girl named Rhonda from the Hope Club. She was super nice. She took me to all my classes and introduced me to all my teachers."

"Oh, that, Rhonda. She is a good girl. You know, Hillary is in the Hope Club. If you want, she can take you instead."

I pulled the blanket tighter with my left hand while still holding the fishing rod. "No. That's okay. I like Rhonda." Peggy had no idea what a monster Hillary was.

"Yes, but Hillary is your sister."

"Please," I begged.

"Okay. Rhonda is nice enough. Anyway, how was the rest of the day?"

I wanted to share so much with Peggy, like how I knew the ethnicity of people when I studied their faces. I wanted to tell her how easy every class was. I recall everything the teachers taught in extensive detail, but I didn't tell Peggy any of it.

It took less than five minutes for me to catch my first fish. Peggy had me do everything: setting the hook, reeling it in, and putting it on a stringer. My fingers wanted to fall off from the cold, frigid water.

I heard Mrs. Jennings's voice in my head. "ATP is a molecule that carries energy within cells."

Could I accelerate the process of energy and make my hands warm? I imagined ATP carrying heat into every one of my hand's cells.

"Ahhh!" I screamed. Instantly, my hands burned. I expected to see them covered in flames, but they looked normal from the outside. -but on the inside. *Mercy me!*

Peggy jumped. "Jane, what is going on? Did you see something?"

"No. My hands are just really hot. Oh, oh, they burn."

Peggy picked up my hands.

"Oh, those feel good. They are like a heat pack."

I concentrated on scaling back some of the ATP, and my hands cooled to a warm instead of boiling.

"That blanket is doing its job in keeping you warm. If they are too hot, just dip them in the water."

"I'm fine."

After fishing for an hour, we returned the four-wheeler and filled the shed's freezer with fish. When I went to my bedroom, I found Alashia and Nina sleeping in my bed. Jill curled in her blankets on the floor. Disappointed, I went down to find Rhett sprawled on the couch, chatting away on his phone.

Where am I going to sleep?

I remembered seeing a camping cot in the shed. I went back to the shed and lay on the stiff cot. The quietness felt peaceful, unlike the chaos of the house. *Maybe I'll make this my new room. No one would bug me here.*

As I enjoyed the serenity, my stomach growled. I rubbed my bones that seemed to poke through my skin. I had gotten skinnier since I came to the Sanibel's. Dinner time was a joke. I had to hand it to Peggy. She made magnificent meals. I loved everything she cooked. She just didn't make enough for a family of fourteen in addition to half of the neighborhood. No one dared steal food off my plate, but I only got small portions. I never felt full.

Cold air blew into my face as I opened the freezer and looked at all the fish. For some reason, Peggy never cooked it. I took out one of the fish we had just caught. I searched the shed for something to cook it on. In the corner, I found a pan in a pile of random odd ends but no heat source. I returned the fish to the freezer and sat on the cot.

If I sleep out here, how will I wake up in time for school?

A clock came into my mind, and I pictured setting it to wake me up at 5:45. I shivered and turned my thin blanket into a cocoon. It didn't have enough bulk to warm me from the cold night. I thought about how I had heated my hands on the boat and concentrated on sending ATP to my whole body. I regulated it until I felt toasty and warm.

Then inspiration hit me. "I can create heat!" I shouted as I threw the cover off me. I ran to the freezer and grabbed the fish. I put the pan on the cement and focused on bringing the energy surrounding me into the pan and heating it up.

Instantly, the fish sizzled.

"Mercy, me," I shouted, using Peggy's catchphrase.

A simple joy filled me as I ate the entire fish. I was surprised about all the bones I had to fish out of my mouth, but it was worth it.

"I'll never have to be hungry again."

———— ◉ ————

IT WAS ALMOST TIME for the bell to ring, and most of the students had their heads on their desks as the teacher droned on. "Nerves transmit thought to action. If you think, 'I am going to move my knee,' the neurons send the message. To do this, they use axons and dendrites." I think the rest of the class had endured all the science they could handle for the day.

Not me. I thought of myself as a sponge, soaking in every lecture Mrs. Jennings had to give. It seemed that each piece of information she presented flipped a switch in me, and I not only remembered the material, but I had complete charts and understanding appear in my head, like thoughts coming out of cold storage.

"What would happen if you interrupted the signal, maybe through an interruption in an axon or dendrite?" She looked around the class, but no one answered. "Then you have lost action potential, and the muscles cannot respond. Do you remember me teaching you about the Mylon sheaths? In multiple sclerosis, these insulators of the cells have eroded, and the brain can no longer send the message to the muscles."

DING.

The bell rang, and everyone bolted out of the classroom. I wasn't ready for the lecture to end. My soul burned fire as Mrs. Jennings flamed my intellect.

Rhonda came up to me.

"Jane, Nancy told me to bring you to the office after science class." My heart raced at her words.

Rhonda looped her arm through mine and started skipping toward the office. Usually, she dragged me, but this time I matched her stride.

"Look at you, Jane! You are skipping!" She said in a voice one might say to a toddler who walked for the first time.

"Hi, ladies," Nancy greeted us as we went into the office. "Thank you, Rhonda."

"Sure thing, Nancy."

Rhonda skipped out.

"Hi, Jane. I hope your foster mom told you we would give you a series of tests over the next few days."

Blah, not more testing!

"The teachers have been watching you, and no one knows if you understand the content."

Oh, I understood. My heart pounded in my chest. I wished Peggy would have warned me about the tests. Nancy left me in a room with a pile of tests and instructions.

I didn't want to take them, so I didn't. I laid my head on the desk and took a nap. The stupid bell kept waking me up, but then I would go back to sleep. Eventually, Rhonda rescued me for lunch, but after, she returned me to the testing room.

The next day at school, Rhonda took me to the testing room again. There Peggy stood, with her lips pierced tight. The school had once again dragged her away from her soaps. I didn't know much about Peggy, but I knew she didn't respond well to this.

What is Peggy doing here? Peggy didn't look up at me from the table.

The principal stood up and extended his hand. I kept my hands tightly over my stomach.

"Hello, Jane. I am Dr. Schmidt, the principal, and it is about time we meet. I have heard so much about you."

Sure, you have. Like I am the poor little girl they found tied up.

Peggy sat in her housecoat fuming. She obviously hadn't brushed her frizzy hair, as it puffed everywhere. She hated being taken from her daytime TV.

"We are concerned. We had planned on testing Jane for three days, but she didn't even try to answer one question. Do you think she can read?"

Peggy shrugged. "Why don't you ask Jane."

Dr. Schmidt looked at me. "Can you read?"

I looked away.

"Mrs. Sanibel, I heard a rumor that Jane only speaks Russian. That would explain a lot of things if that were more than a rumor."

Peggy glared at me. "I don't know if she speaks Russian, but she speaks English fluently."

Dr. Schmidt let out a nervous laugh. "Oh, that's good." He turned to me. "Jane, no one reports you talking at school. Can you tell me why you don't talk here?" He ran his hand up the side of his face and stared at me.

I looked at Peggy to save me. I should have known better. She didn't rescue anyone.

"Jane, please sit down." Dr. Schmidt pulled out a chair next to Peggy. I sat by her and noticed her red aura. No doubt she hated me for pulling her away from home. Would all those little kids be safe unsupervised?

Dr. Schmidt carried on.

I had noticed that most happy people had a violet aura, so I concentrated and turned mine violet. Happy emotions flowed in me, and I couldn't hold back the smile. When Peggy saw my joy, she scowled at me, so I imagined sending my aura to her. *Wouldn't it be great if she was happy?* To my surprise, it worked. I watched as my colors mixed with hers and changed her aura to violet.

Peggy did a 180 transformation as a smile transformed her face. Dr. Schmidt kept spewing words behind his yellow-green aura. I sent my violet light bands to him, and after the colors intermingled, Dr. Schmidt's aura turned purple. He also took on a huge smile.

"Dr. Schmidt," Peggy said, interrupting the principal. "A bridge went to bridge school and did something wrong. He was called into the principal's office, and the principal then said you're suspended."

Dr. Schmidt burst into laughter, and Peggy joined in. I couldn't help it, and a few snickers escaped me, even though the joke wasn't funny.

"I got another one. On a Monday morning, a mother went in to wake up her son. Wake up, son. It's time to go to school! But Mom, I don't want to go. The mom said, give me two reasons why. The son said, well, the kids hate me, and the teachers hate me too! Then the mom said, that's no reason. Come now, get ready. Then the son said, give me two reasons why I should go. And the mom replied, well, for one, you are 52 years old. And for another, you're the principal!".

I laughed. That one was funny. Dr. Schmidt pounded his thigh with his hand as snot ran out of his face.

I think violet is my new favorite color.

⎯⎯⎯⎯ ◆ ⎯⎯⎯⎯

IT BEGAN THE USUAL way. We cast our lines out as Athena curled into my lap. The air seemed warmer, and I felt comfortable.

"Jane, why do you not speak to others? I have been watching you at home. The kids desperately want to be friends with their new sister, but you block them out."

I pulled the blanket under my chin. *I don't want to talk about this.*

"The meeting with the school principal didn't go well. You lock yourself away from the teachers. Jane, what can I do to convince you to start talking to others?"

I wanted to go mute on Peggy. I petted Athena to escape the conversation.

"Oh no, you don't. Don't go all mute on me."

I kept my eyes on Athena. "I don't know. I guess it is because I feel stupid. I am supposed to be this teenager here, yet I feel like a toddler is smarter than me. If I don't talk, then no one will know how dumb I am."

"The more you don't talk, the more dumb people *think you are.* Everyone knows you had a hard past. They don't expect brilliance from you. They want to get to know who Jane Doe is."

"About my name..."

"Yes."

My throat tightened. "I hate it."

"Why so?"

"It isn't a real name."

"What makes you think that?"

Hillary tells me almost daily. "Some of the kids at school tease me about it."

"Are things not going well for you at school?"

It's such a tricky question. "Rhonda is good to include me in things, but no one talks to me."

"That's because they know you won't respond. Teen years are so hard anyway. Every kid there is struggling to define themselves socially. Believe it or not, most are just as scared as you, but they hide it. It takes a lot to put yourself out there socially. When you don't talk to them, then you reject them, and they feel vulnerable and stupid. So yeah, as long as you play the dumb mute kid, they will leave you in that sphere."

I remembered all the cruel tauntings as my heart ached. The crisp air tingled my nose, but I loved how fresh everything smelt on the reservoir. But my peer's hateful words filled my head.

"Rhonda, aren't you done dragging this stupid girl around? When does your assignment end?"

"Jane Doe. That is like John Doe. They give that name to nobodies."

"They must have cut off Jane's tongue in the Russian's basement."

"The Russians chemically wiped out her personality."

"How would it feel to be dumb like Jane?"

Peggy took my hands in hers. "Oh, wow, your hands are warm." I loved my new ability. "Anyways, Jane, you can change this. Start talking to people. Show them who Jane is."

"I don't know who Jane is."

"Well, show them. You are super lucky right now. As we go through life, people quickly label us, and it is hard to break that label. For instance, Christian is super hyper. -super hyper! Lots of kids can't stand him. He carries that label. Sometimes, Christian becomes serious and has great ideas to share, but no one will listen because they don't take him seriously. He will have to work really hard to break that label. But you, you have no label."

"Yes, I do. I am labeled stupid."

"That is because no one knows you. This label you can quickly remove if you show people who you are. Everyone is superbly interested in you, and the moment you show them who you are, they will accept that."

"But I don't know who I am."

A fish tightened my line.

"Alora, you got one!"

I yanked my pole, and the line went slack.

"It got away," I said.

"Oh well. Reel it in and see if it took your bait."

As I reeled my line, Peggy continued. "It's kind of cool that you don't know who you are. You have a chance to become anyone you want to be. You are a blank slate without bad habits. I suggest you do two things. Read lots of books on how to win friends. Read books on how to cultivate relationships. The other thing I suggest is for you to write down all the qualities you wish to have, then make them Jane."

"Can I change my name?"

"I don't know why not. How about Samantha? I always planned on naming my twelfth kid Samantha, or Sam, if it were a boy."

"No."

"Let's see. There is Karen, Joletta, Spring, Summer, Margo, Stacy, Janice, Candice, Lilly, Erin."

"No."

"Do you have a name you are considering?"

"Alora Funk."

"ALORA FUNK! What a strange name. Why that name?"

"Maybe it was my name before. It just keeps playing in my mind."

"Interesting. If you think Alora Funk is your name, then, by all means, you should use it."

Alora Funk.

Yes.

I wanted it. It was better than Jane Doe, even if it weren't my real name.

"Jane...I mean Alora. -Alora, that is going to take some getting used to. Anyways, Alora, I will give you a notebook when we get home, and I want you to start defining Alora Funk. I want you to write in it everything you wish you were, then become it. Plus, go to your school library and find books that can help you to socialize with people. Also, I want you to start talking to people besides me."

I could be anyone I wanted to be. Who did I want to be? My nerves vibrated at the thought of creating myself. I hadn't thought of that.

As we walked into the house, we heard a crash.

I followed Peggy and found broken glass scattered over the kitchen floor.

"Who did this?" Peggy screamed.

No one answered.

"I don't know why no one is in bed. This is way past your bedtime. Everyone gets to bed now while I clean this up!"

Hillary snapped back, "I can't wait to graduate, and then I will move as far away from this dump. Of course, it wouldn't matter if I moved across the world. I will still be able to hear your yelling." Hillary rubbed her nose and then said, 2020 can't get here soon enough."

The rest of the kids ignored Peggy. -something they were good at doing. They went on with their activities as if she weren't there. Besides, what did she mean by bedtime? The Sanibel kids always stayed up late. I doubt they had a concept of bedtime. I stood in the living room, not sure what to do.

Peggy came out of the kitchen with a towel wrapped around her right hand. -bright blood soaked through the towel.

"Wait, I need everyone to come here." She clanged the dinner bell, and most of the family soon gathered in the living room.

When everyone was there, Peggy said," What do you say to broken glass? Rest in pieces!"

"Seriously, you got me out of bed for that?" Corbon said.

Peggy opened the towel and looked at her bleeding hand. "I wanted to lighten the mood. Before we go to bed, Jane has something she wants to say."

I do?

All eyes stared at me. This wasn't exactly how I planned on sharing my voice. I had no idea what I should say. My legs started shaking.

Finally, I reached deep inside my diaphragm and said, "My name is Alora Funk."

⸺⸺●⸺⸺

AFTER MOST OF THE FAMILY was in bed, I went to the kitchen to get a drink of water. The broken glass sat on the top of the garbage. Peggy had cut herself pretty good on it, and it had taken her a while to stop the bleeding. Too bad it was my favorite butterfly cup that had broken.

"Everything is made up of molecules," Mrs. Jennings had taught us. "Alchemy was popular at the end of the seventeenth century. People believed that they could change anything into something else. During the eighteenth century, however..."

I picked up a piece of broken glass with a pink butterfly wing coloring on it.

This cup is molecules. What would it take to put it back together?

I imagined the pieces of glass coming together. As I did, a miraculous thing happened in the garbage can. All the glass shards came together, and the cup became whole!

I picked the butterfly cup out of the garbage and examined it. I couldn't find any seems or lines where the glass had fused. I traced my hand over the smooth glass.

"Who is Alora Funk?"

ANXIETY OVERWHELMED me. *Can I really talk to the kids at school?* Spots flashed in my eyes at the thought. *What if I say something stupid?*

We passed a sign in the hall that said, "Twenty-five-dollar reward to anyone who turns in information on the vandalization of the school."

I would like twenty-five-dollars.

Rhonda and I reached the office. "Well, have fun with your counselor." She said as she turned and walked away.

"Thank you.," I squeaked out. Rhonda spun around and ran back to me.

"Did you just talk?" Her eyes widened, and she looked confused.

"Yes. I wanted to." My mouth went dry. "To thank you for all the nice things you have done for me." I held my shaking hands behind my back. I wished I hadn't said anything. What if she pressed me to talk more?

Rhonda lurched into a hug. I liked touch and probably lingered too long. She pushed away.

"You don't have a Russian accent."

I brought my hands forward. "No."

"Why haven't you talked until now?"

I shrugged as I bit my fingernails. Yup, I knew the questions would flow once I shared my voice.

"Well, don't stop talking. This is great. Everyone will be so happy to learn you can talk." With that, Rhonda skipped away.

I went into the counselor's room and sat across from Marge, my counselor.

"Sit down, Jane." I met with her three times a week. I sat while she kept her eyes on the computer. "Give me just a sec. I have something I need to finish up." Marge tapped at the keys for ten more minutes, then turned to me.

"I have something fun we are going to do today." She put a large piece of white paper and a box of markers in front of me. "I would like you to draw a picture of yourself. You aren't getting graded, so don't stress about it. Just draw who you are."

I opened the box of markers and picked out the blue one, which was the closest shade to my brilliant blue aura. I felt comfortable with Marge. Out of everyone, she was the only person who took the greatest interest in me. Well, I guess Peggy, but she was a hard one. Unless we were on the boat together, she didn't notice me. She didn't see anyone, really, consumed in her world.

I drew two large eyes in the center of the paper. Marge had returned to typing on her computer. When I finished, I returned the markers and waited for Marge to acknowledge it. She seemed engrossed by whatever she was typing.

Eventually, I said, "Done."

Marge jumped in her seat and turned to me.

"You spoke!"

My cheeks went warm, and I popped the lid on and off the marker multiple times. Marge reigned in her enthusiasm as she picked up my paper.

"Oh, that is very lovely. Can you tell me about it?"

"That is me fishing at the reservoir."

Marge's eyes moistened. "It is so lovely. But, do you want to know what is more lovely than that?"

I shrugged.

"Hearing your voice."

I looked away when Peggy's words came into my head. "You need to look people in their eyes." I returned my gaze to Marge. It was hard to hold as my eyes threatened to rebel and look away.

"Can you tell me more about the picture?"

"That's it."

She studied the picture and then asked, "What made you share your voice with me today?"

"You feel safe," I said.

What a stupid answer.

"I am glad you feel that way. I am safe. You can trust me with anything."

"Can you help me with something?"

"Anything. Well, anything within reason."

"My name is Alora Funk, not Jane Doe. Can you help me change it with the teachers?"

"Oh yes, Alora. That is a beautiful name. I am glad you are sharing it with me."

She handed me back my picture. "Is there anything you would like to talk about?"

I shrugged. She looked at her watch.

"Well, it's almost your lunchtime. Remember, I am always here if you want to talk." She scribbled something on a sticky note and handed it to me. "I know you probably have lots of things stored inside you that you don't know how to deal with. This is my cellphone number. If you ever need to talk to me, please call. I don't care what time of night it is. I am here for you."

I took her phone number as the bell rang.

"Make good choices," she said.

I went into the front office and saw Rhonda laughing with Nancy. Rhonda came to my side. "Jane, you ready for lunch?"

Marge stood behind me. "Tell her your name."

I took a deep breath as my shoulders rose and dropped. "My name is Alora Funk."

Rhonda clapped, and Nancy joined in.

"Well, let's go to lunch, Alora!"

Rhonda looped her arm in mine and skipped to lunch. I didn't skip this time as my head became light, and I felt like I might puke again. *What will all the kids think when I talk?*

Once we sat down with our trays, Rhonda stood back up.

"Hey guys, guess what? My friend Jane here has something she wants to tell you."

All eyes turned to me.

What did I want to tell them?

She nudged me.

"My name is Alora Funk."

"She can talk!"

"Did you hear her?'

"Alora Funk is way better than Jane Doe."

"She doesn't sound Russian."

Rhonda put her arm over my shoulders. "That's exactly what I thought."

"Why haven't you talked to us?"

"Whoa, guys. Let's give Alora some space." Rhonda said. I felt warmth for her for sticking up for me, demanding that I got space. I needed it.

I kept my eyes on my food as I ate, and the food turned to cement in my stomach. Soon, everyone's attention turned to the latest gossip, and once again, I was forgotten. At that moment, I preferred it that way.

———◦———

MY TOLERANCE GAVE OUT. Like every weekend, the house shook from chaos. The Sanibels and all their friends ran around and fought. I needed peace, so I went outside.

Why did Peggy want to bring me into their home, one more child for her to ignore and one more to add to the chaos?

I went outside, and the sun shone brightly and warmed my skin. A light breeze filled me with smells of pollen.

It's 72 degrees out here.

How did I know that? I just did.

I went to the campground in the area and explored it. How would I ever get the Sanibels to take me camping? I wandered across the street to the reservoir. A few early morning fishermen fished along the shoreline. Their soft conversation drifted to me. I sat on a giant boulder and dipped my feet into the water. My toes curled inward as cold water sent electric shocks up my legs. Birds trilled in stereo as I took a stick and swirled the water. The reservoir had a way of removing the madness that clung to me from living with the Sanibels. The man to my right fought with his line to real in his latest catch. Next time, I would have to bring a pole and try fishing from the rocks. My feet numbed to the cold, and I brought them out and put my shoes back on.

From beneath the rocks, a rat came out with a body as large as a cat.

"Ahh!" I screamed as I jumped up, and my fear echoed across the water. The anglers looked at me for a moment and went back to fishing. The rat's whiskers twitched as he studied me.

"Go on," I said, waving my stick his way. White bubbles foamed around his mouth. Instead of fearing me, as I suspected he would, he came at me. I suppressed screaming as I stumbled backward, still waving my stick. This rat seemed to want to take me on.

He has rabies!

We had learned in science that animals with rabies don't fear predators as they usually would. The virus makes them aggressive. A hiss came from the vermin. I grabbed a rock and chucked it at the rat but missed. He ran toward me, his yellow teeth glistening. I tried to run backward, keeping my eye on him, then tripped. My stick flew out of my hand. The rat rushed toward my leg. I no longer had a weapon. I couldn't see any rocks small enough to grab.

Alora, do something!

As the rat reached my leg, I thought about axons, dendrites, and Mylon sheaths. I concentrated on sending the signal to his body to halt the transmission of information. I imagined all his axons being blocked and his Mylon sheaths unraveling. The rat opened his mouth wider and went to sink his teeth into me. *Bam!* With its mouth open, the rat stopped and remained stiff and unmoving, his teeth touching my skin. It had worked! I had blocked him, hadn't I? He instantly seemed like a statue and not a living creature.

I crawled away and then watched him. He didn't move. Had I really stopped the transfer of information in the rat?

I searched the rocks until I found another long stick. I poked it at the rat, and the grotesque thing fell onto its side, still not moving.

I had done it. I had stopped his nerves from functioning, making him paralyzed!

I scrambled up the rocks to the hill above. Feeling safe from the rat, I concentrated on restarting his neurons. He stood on all fours and sniffed the rocks, having his neuron functions restored. I ran toward home before he remembered me.

In the yard, I breathed heavily as my chest moved up and down. Little drops of sweat dripped into my eyes, and the salt felt like it was melting them.

Had that just happened? Had I done that?

"Athena!" I called, looking for companionship. The dog was nowhere to be found. I headed back toward the reservoir, but my legs carried me in another direction, with my mind still thinking about the rat. I walked until I came to the highway. Fast cars sped past, blasting me with wind. Small particles went into my eyes, and I madly rubbed them until they felt better.

I looked at the highway. If I turned left, I would leave the canyon and end up in Brigham City, where my school was.

What is up the canyon?

Curious and bored, I walked along the shoulder of the highway. It had been over two months since I moved in with the Sanibels. Things seemed to be going well. I was talking more at home. I started hanging out with Alashia and Christian. We often played games or drew. Christian seemed to settle down when he drew, but when he wasn't, that boy was crazy. I smiled, thinking about him. He often took us on adventures in the yard.

As I walked, butterflies flew around me. Despite the loud cars, I heard the sweet song of birds. I even saw a fox dive into the bushes. After walking a mile, I heard rocks crunching as a car pulled behind me. I jumped close to the bushes, afraid the car would hit me.

"Hey, girl," a voice came. I turned and saw a rusty blue car with three teens inside.

I wanted to leap into the bushes, but there wasn't room for me.

Am I in trouble?

"Every time you meet someone, do it confidently," Peggy's words echoed in my head.

I can do this.

"Yes," I said, choking on the layer of grit in my mouth.

"Come here."

I walked to the passenger side of the car. A boy with long, greasy hair had his head out of the window.

"What's your name?"

I looked at him, then at the driver. They seemed several years older than me. "Alora Funk."

The boy stuck his hand out to me. "I am Tom!"

"Always shake a hand extended to you," Peggy's words continued. I took Tom's hand.

"Wanna go for a ride?"

My feet bounced under me as my legs shook. Did I want to go for a ride? Should I go? No one had ever told me what to do in a situation like that.

"Sure."

Did I do the right thing?

Both passenger doors opened. Tom came out of the front, and a girl with dreadlocks came out of the back. "My name is Liz," the girl said. She sat in the front seat, and Tom took my hand.

My heart raced to his touch. "You can sit in the back with me."

I climbed in the back with Tom. The heavy smoke in the car burned my eyes and felt like the cologne from the strange people back at the hospital. My lungs wanted to cough like they had at the hospital, but I suppressed it.

The driver leaned back. "I am Joe. You ready for some fun?"

I didn't answer. Joe's tires squealed as he pulled onto the highway. He quickly gained speed as he passed every car we came to, weaving through the traffic more aggressively than Mr. Scary had. The only difference was Joe wasn't angry like Mr. Scary. Everyone in the car had lime-green auras. Mine was the color of fear, icy blue.

Tom scooted close to me and put his arm over my shoulders. "Thanks for coming. I am like the third wheel here."

Liz and Joe laughed, engaged in their conversation.

"Tell me about yourself, Alora."

"I don't know what to say."

"What school do you go to?"

"ACYI."

Tom took his arm off my shoulders. "You are a baby." His forehead creased, and he looked at his friends. He whispered to me, "That's okay. I don't mind 'em young. Just don't tell those guys. If they ask how old you are, tell them you are sixteen and homeschooled. You would do that for me, babe?"

Babe?

It felt like little bugs crawled on my skin; simultaneously, an alarm in my subconscious rang violently.

I probably shouldn't be here.

Tom relaxed into me again.

After we left the canyon, we drove along fields and into the city of Logan, and everything seemed so green. Logan had many shops and traffic, much bigger than Mantua or Brigham City. Before I knew it, we were driving through another canyon. I kept wanting to ask them to take me home. Fear consumed me. I had no idea where we were going.

I stayed reasonably quiet most of the drive, but my new friends didn't. They had the energy of Christian. And for some reason, everything was funny to them. They laughed in hysterics at almost anything.

"You are so quiet," Tom said to me.

"I don't know what to say."

"Tell us a joke."

I knew a thousand jokes from Peggy.

"Let's see. What did one traffic light say to the other? Stop looking at me, I'm changing!"

Everyone laughed and laughed. Usually, no one laughed at Peggy's jokes, and yet I made them laugh. Was it really that funny?

"That's good. Tell us another one."

"Why did the gym close down? It just didn't work out!"

Again, they burst into laughter.

"You are so funny."

I kept going, afraid I would have to tell them something about me if I stopped. "Want to hear a construction joke? Oh, never mind, I'm still working on that one."

I kept spilling out jokes, and they responded vigorously. That helped me relax. I had never gotten such positive responses from anyone. Maybe I should put a comedian on the list of attributes I wanted Alora to have.

"Look, there is Bear Lake," Joe said. I looked out the windshield and saw the most magnificent turquoise-blue lake. We had reached the summit and were looking down into paradise. Mantua Reservoir seemed like a puddle compared to the shimmery lake. I couldn't see all of Bear Lake, but I surmised it stretched out for miles.

"Have you ever been to Bear Lake?" Tom asked.

"No."

"They call it the Caribbean of the Rocky Mountains."

Liz said, "It does look like the Caribbean. I went on a cruise there last summer. But it isn't warm like the Caribbean. Bear Lake is like swimming in Antarctica."

"Sure is."

For the moment, the majestic view of Bear Lake made me forget my trepidation. We drove into the valley and stopped at a convenient station to satisfy everyone's "munchies". Tom bought me a slushie and hotdog. As we acted like adults, I felt a freedom spark within. The easy smile on my face started becoming more natural.

We took our treats and went to a small cabin next to the lake.

Tom asked, "Remind me again who this cabin belongs to?"

Liz said, "It's my grandma's. Remember, she doesn't know we are here, so we must leave it like we found it."

Joe crossed his arms. "I was expecting something bigger," he said.

"Beggars can't be choosers. If you don't like it, go rent a hotel."

Liz retrieved a hidden key out of the bush next to the door. We walked in, and the smell of stale mildew hit us. The tiny cabin seemed smaller inside with the darkness. Liz opened all the blinds, and bright sun rays filled the front room. White dust particles seemed to sparkle in the sun's rays.

"Who's ready to swim?"

Swim? Panic tensed my muscles. Did I know how to swim? I didn't even have a swimsuit.

Everyone dug through their bags and pulled out their suits and towels. Liz must have seen the uncertainty on my face.

"Don't worry...What was your name again?"

"Alora."

"Don't worry. In the bedroom, Grandma has a drawer full of swimsuits you can borrow. I hope you don't mind wearing a used suit. She cleans them."

All I had ever known was used clothing. One of my worries disappeared after being given a suit, but I still fretted over swimming.

After we changed, Liz came screaming from the bathroom. "Where is my necklace?"

The guys shrugged. She looked at me.

How am I supposed to know?

"Did you take it, Alora?" The tension in the room felt almost as uncomfortable as my first day of school when Hilary had dragged me into her classroom, and I had puked in front of everyone.

My heart sped up. I hadn't taken it. Why would she think I had?

"No," I said in a weak voice that sounded more like a liar.

Liz's face reddened. "That necklace is an heirloom. It is worth probably ten thousand dollars. This is not cool. I need it back."

Everyone turned to me as if expecting me to hand it over and apologize. I didn't know where to look or what to say. Liz went back into the bathroom to search again. She came out with a more perplexed look on her face.

"One of you has stolen it. Listen, I won't be mad if it suddenly appears. So, whoever has it, before we leave, put it back."

We stood in a silence that felt like a death sentence. I know I hadn't stolen it. Tom looked as pale and nervous as I felt.

"Alright, let's go swim," Joe said, breaking the tension.

"We have all sorts of beach toys in the shed," Liz said, but she no longer acted free-spirited. What were the chances that she hadn't even brought the necklace?

We dragged the toys to the beach. Joe and Liz immediately had a wrestling match in the water. Tom turned to me, looking like he wanted the same. I quickly grabbed the kayak and pulled it into the water to avoid such a thing.

Instantly, my toes turned into rectangle ice cubes. Liz hadn't been kidding when she said the water felt like Antarctica. I jumped into the kayak and rowed away from Tom. I hadn't kayaked before but had seen plenty of people do it on the reservoir. It didn't take long for me to get the hang of it.

After about twenty minutes, Joe swam over to me. "Hey, don't hog the kayak." The kayak had been my safety net, and I wasn't ready to leave it, but what choice did I have? I slipped into the water, and the icy cold took my breath away. I used my mind to create energy and warm myself, and then I tried to swim.

I was surprised to find the water went out a long way before it ever got deep. I eventually allowed myself to dog-paddle around. Whenever Tom came close, I would duck underwater and move away—no wrestling match for him.

We hadn't been in the water for two hours when large clouds blocked the sun. Almost instantly, the intense cold of the water overwhelmed the others. I didn't feel cold since I had sent my ATP all through my body, keeping myself warm.

"I think it's time to go in," Joe said as his teeth chattered, and his lips went blue.

"Yes!"

Yay! I had escaped having to water-wrestle with Tom.

After we returned the beach gear, Tom put his arm over my shoulders and walked with me into the house.

"How are you so warm?" He said in a high-pitched tone. "I don't think that I have ever been so cold in my life. Let's go cuddle, and you can warm me up." He licked his lips, and I turned away. "We are going to get a fire going, and you and I can *really get to know each other.*"

I didn't know what he meant, but a creepy feeling entered me. I didn't want to *really get to know Tom.*

Everyone stood wrapped in their towels, shivering as their skin looked blueish-white.

I am glad I know how to keep myself warm.

"Listen, guys," Liz said, coming from the kitchen. "I have just the thing to warm us up."

She held a bottle of Vodka.

No one in the Sanibel house drank alcohol, but I had learned about it in school. I had even signed a contract in health class that I would not drink alcohol or do drugs while in high school. I had no desire to drink.

Tom grabbed the bottle from Liz and took a swig. He came to me and planted a sloppy kiss on my cheek. He held out the bottle. I threw my hands behind my chest, and my breath came out in pulsating shudders.

"This will loosen you up, and then the real fun will begin."

Health class had also warned me that sometimes guys took advantage of girls when they were drunk. I had no doubt Tom had those intentions.

Joe took the bottle as Liz flipped a switch on the gas fireplace, and a yellow fire came to life. Tom put his arm over me again, and his nasty alcoholic breath surrounded my face. "You and me, Babe," he said, winking.

You and me nothing.

Joe held the Vodka to me. "Your turn," he said.

I tried to say no, but no words came. Peer pressure turned out harder than the health teacher had made it out to be. "If you decide beforehand not to drink, then you will have no problem saying no when you are met with peer pressure," the teacher's voice echoed in my head.

"Can I change into dry clothes?" I asked.

"Sure," Liz said. "Everyone, as you change in the bathroom, if, the person who took my necklace would be so kind as to return it. I will change last, and then I will never know who took it." Again, all eyes turned to me.

I don't have your stupid necklace.

Tom took another drink of Vodka and said to me, "I will be out here waiting for you." Again, he winked.

I pushed his arm off me and almost ran to the bathroom. I locked the door and looked at myself in the mirror. I looked like a wet, caged bird.

How have I gotten myself into this situation? I had no idea what to do. I didn't want to find out what Tom had in mind for me. I didn't want to drink. What was I going to do?

I changed my clothes and sat on the toilet, holding myself. Tears streamed out of my eyes.

Pound. Pound Pound. "Girl, hurry up, we are freezing," came Liz's voice.

I went to unlock the door, then stopped. I turned to the window.

Pound. Pound. Pound.

The window squeaked as it opened, but thankfully, it was during the pounding. Hopefully, they didn't hear it.

I quickly crawled out and ran to the road. Cars flew by.

Where am I? Where will I go?

Powerful fear filled me. If I ran, what was my plan? I didn't know where I was other than at a place called Bear Lake. How would I get home?

Maybe I should just go back.

"Where do you think you're going?" Liz's words made me jump. She was right behind me.

I turned and looked at her. She had her fists balled up.

"I never trusted you," she said. "I know what you are doing! You are running away with my necklace."

She lunged at me and grabbed my hair. She yanked so hard that she came away with a handful of it. "Give me my necklace back!"

What do I do? What do I do?

Suddenly, I remembered the rat from earlier. I had blocked its neurons, and he couldn't move. As Liz took another handful of hair, I concentrated on blocking her neurons, which wasn't easy to do with the pain of losing more hair.

Liz froze.

It had worked! I had made her unmovable as I had the rat.

I took off running.

I ran and ran and ran. I quickly slowed down, not used to such exertion. I concentrated on bringing the natural surrounding energy into me. Instantly, I felt rejuvenated and ran some more. Meanwhile, the sun was close to setting.

Eventually, I saw a gas station. I ducked in and stood by the large windowpanes, panting and crying. The smell of fried food and the store's warmth caught my attention.

The clerk came around the counter to me.

"Is there something wrong?"

I didn't know her. *Should I tell her my situation?* She had kindness on her face, reminding me of Deborah from the crisis nursery. Her golden-yellow aura shone brightly around her. She was my only chance to help.

Without reservation, the entirety of my story was spelled out to her. Well, not the entirety. I left the part out about paralyzing Liz. The clerk fidgeted with her hands as she patiently listened. I couldn't look at her when I finished.

"You did the right thing," she said. At that moment, Joe's rusty blue car pulled into the parking lot. All three of my "new" friends were in it. I felt a little relieved that I hadn't left Liz paralyzed for life because I had wondered if I had. My effects must have worn off, but I was almost paralyzed from fear.

"That is them," I said, shaking. I bit my fingernails so hard that I nicked the tip of my finger. Sharp pain instantly shot into my hand.

"Hurry, duck behind the counter. I won't tell them you are here."

Chapter 4

DING. DING. The bell on the door announced their entry. I could hear them shuffle around the store.

I crouched behind the counter and smacked my elbow on the way down. It throbbed as I tried to suppress calling out in pain.

"Check the bathroom," Liz said.

"Can I help you?" The Clerk said.

I heard Joe's voice. "We're good."

"The bathroom is empty," Tom said.

"Where could she have gone? There is nowhere else to go."

"Maybe she is hiding in the trees along the road."

"When I get ahold of her, I am going to give her a beating she will never forget."

Did Liz realize she was paralyzed, or was that a blank spot in her memory? Too bad I couldn't ask her.

The Clerk shifted her weight on her legs next to my crouched body. "Can I help you with something?" She said again.

"Listen, Lady, we are fine!" Liz snapped.

"I don't support loiters. Buy something or leave."

The three whispered, but I couldn't make out what they said.

"If you don't leave, I will call the cops." The Clerk said.

Ding. Ding. Either someone new came in, or they left.

"They are gone but stay down. They are still in the parking lot. I will tell you when they leave.

Eternity looped around me twice before they left. The Clerk reached down and pulled me up.

"How are you doing?" she asked. I hadn't realized how much my arms were shaking. I tried to hold them and steady myself.

A fierce pressure built up in my stomach, and I worried I might puke like I had in class.

"You can use my phone to call your parents."

"Thank you," I said. She pulled a phone up to the counter. I looked at it. Who would I call? I didn't know the Sanibel's phone number.

I thought of Marge's number.

"Will you dial it for me? It's 345-555-4679."

The Clerk's forehead wrinkled as she dialed the number and handed me the phone.

"Hello," I heard through the phone.

I went to speak, but my words did not come out.

"Hello."

"Um, Marge?"

"This is her."

"Hey, I am sorry to bother you." A term I heard Peggy use all the time. "This is Alora Funk." My voice choked up. "I am in a bit of trouble, and I don't know what to do." As I spoke, my voice sounded foreign to me.

"Alora, hi. What is going on?"

"Well, I had taken a ride with some teenagers I didn't know, and they brought me to Bear Lake. Do you know where I am?"

"I know where Bear Lake is."

"Well, they weren't good kids. They were drinking, and I snuck away. Now, I am stuck here and don't know what to do." I couldn't believe how much my voice shook, and the tears flowed as I spoke.

"Do your parents know where you are?"

"No."

"Why don't you call them?"

How can I call them without their number? "I can't."

There was silence.

"Well, Alora, I want you to know you did the right thing. It isn't easy saying no to peer pressure. I am proud of you. What can I do for you?"

My throat tightened as the tears broke through again. "I don't know where I am. I don't know what to do."

The Clerk watched me with eyes that felt kind yet judgmental.

There was silence, then I heard Marge say, "Tell me where you are at, and I will come get you."

"I am at Bear Lake."

"But where?"

I looked at the Clerk. "She wants to know where I am at Bear Lake."

"Hand me the phone, and I will tell her."

After I hung up the phone, the Clerk asked, "Would you like something to eat?"

"I don't have any money."

"Don't worry about that. Go grab yourself something to eat."

Honestly, my stomach hurt. I didn't want food. I didn't move.

"Well, go on, get yourself something."

I wandered around the store and returned to the counter with a bottle of Sprite.

"You need more than that." The Clerk took a slice of pizza out of the heating case and handed it to me.

A few customers came and went as I waited for Marge. Thankfully, the teens never returned. I watched outside as dark took over. Finally, Marge arrived.

I ran into her arms, and she embraced me with the most comforting hug. Again, the tears poured out, and my head pounded.

"Thank you," Marge told the Clerk.

"Yes, thank you," I said.

"You did the right thing, kid. I just wish all kids were as smart as you."

Smart! I am not smart. I shouldn't have gotten into their car.

We climbed into Marge's car, but she didn't start it. She handed me her phone.

"Please call your parents. They are going to be worried about you."

I wasn't sure about that.

"I don't know their phone number."

Marge took her phone and searched on it for a while. "I can't find their number." She said, putting her phone down. "Listen, I am not comfortable driving through two canyons at night. There are a lot of deer around, and it isn't safe. We are going to have to get a hotel room. I hope that is okay with you. Man, I wish we could at least let your parents know."

⸺⸺◉⸺⸺

MARGE LOCKED THE HOTEL room, and finally, I felt safe. What a day that had been. I was almost bitten by a rabid rat and beaten by a girl. -not to forget the advances of Tom and the peer pressure. And everything! It had been too much.

Quickly, I climbed into bed. I had forgotten how soft beds were since I only slept on the cot in the shed. I buried myself in the blankets and instantly fell asleep.

We left early in the morning since Marge was anxious to get me home. She stopped in Logan to get gas and returned to the car with a present for me.

"I bought you a bracelet."

She handed me a delicate string of colorful beads. I blinked at her in surprise and shock as she secured it on my wrist. This was the first time anyone had bought me anything nice. I fingered the beads on the rest of the ride home. I would cherish the bracelet forever.

When we pulled into my driveway, she turned off the car. "Can I come in with you and explain the situation to your parents?" She asked.

I shrugged. As we walked across the yard, Athena appeared and jumped onto Marge.

"Down, Athena," I shouted. Athena ignored me. I grabbed her collar and pulled her off Marge. We walked inside, and an eerie silence greeted us. I had never heard this place silent.

Marge followed me around the house, but no one was there. Then I recalled it was Sunday.

"I think they are at church," I said.

"Okay. Well, can I do anything else for you?"

"No." I threw myself into her arms and gave her a long hug.

"Listen, if your parents have any questions, then please call me."

"Okay."

"I really wish I could have spoken with them. Are you going to be okay?"

I nodded.

"Alora," she said, pulling the hair out of my eyes. My head stung where Liz had attacked.

"My door will always be opened to you. If you ever need me again, please call. And you did the right thing. I am very proud of you."

I watched Marge leave, and a part of me wanted to go with her. I slumped onto the floor and curled my back against the wall.

After some time passed, I made myself a bowl of cereal and sat at the table. The muffin I ate at the hotel was long gone, and my stomach ached for food. As I ate, the Sanibels came home.

Everyone filed past me but Peggy. "You missed church," she snapped. I looked at my cereal. "Don't get in the habit of missing church. It is the most important part of your week." With that, she left.

Do they know I have been gone? Doesn't she realize I didn't even sleep here last night?

They hadn't noticed.

I felt shame for my naivety. I was relieved not to have to tell them my story, yet having them so unaware of me left a lonely feeling deep within.

MY THROAT DRIED AS she explained the assignment. Perhaps I breathed more heavily through my mouth because of it.

"Isn't it exciting? You are the class of 2020! What a terrific year to graduate." Mrs. Palmer, the English teacher, said. 2020 seemed forever away.

Hillary raised her hand. I hated having English with her since she always tried to be the center of attention. "I am leaving this town as soon as I graduate. Maybe I will go to New York City or California."

No one cares!

I doodled in my notebook as the teacher taught. "This is important. Pay attention," Mrs. Palmer said. I looked up. "You will create a PowerPoint presentation and present it to the class. To receive full points, you must follow the rubrics."

PowerPoint? What did she mean?

Mrs. Palmer allowed me to come in during lunches so she could teach me how to make a PowerPoint presentation. Creating one wasn't as hard as I thought, but imagining myself presenting it in front of the class terrified me.

When I got home, I asked Peggy, "Is there a computer and a flash drive I can use?"

"Yeah, there are some hanging around somewhere."

"Where?"

Peggy peeled potatoes and seemed to make a pie crust simultaneously. Steam boiled from the pan, and Peggy's hair went extra frizzy.

"I don't know! Just look around. The tables. The kids' bedrooms. You'll find something somewhere." She snapped at me as if I had interrupted a soap opera.

After searching the main floor, I wandered to the bedrooms. Hillary had a shelf connected to her bed, and I crawled on her mattress to explore it. On it was a box with painted bright red letters, "PRIVATE! DO NOT OPEN!" The box had a digital lock, keeping it secure. I heard a bunch of girls in the bedroom next door, but no one was in this room. What type of things would Hillary want to hide from everyone? My fingers traced the lettering as I tried to decipher what number combination Hillary would use.

If I had a secret box, what would I store in it? I didn't have any secrets. Well, maybe my trip to Bear Lake was a secret. I touched the bracelet Marge had given me. She would always have a spot in my heart for her kindness. What would life have been like if she had been my foster mom and not Peggy?

I tried putting the address in the lock, but it did not open. I didn't know Hillary's birthdate, but she was either born in 2001, 2002, or 2003. I tried all three. They didn't work.

"I cannot wait to graduate," Hillary's words echoed in my head. "I will move as far away from this dump," she often said.

I put 2020, our graduation year, into the lock.

It opened.

The lid swung back, and my fingers tingled in anticipation. I glanced over my shoulder to make sure no one watched me. What would Hillary do if she saw me in her secret box? I looked inside, and the buildup dropped.

The only thing in it was a flash drive.

"How stupid," I muttered out loud. I was looking for a treasure or a juicy secret. Maybe a diary I could snoop in. If I had a secret box, I wouldn't keep a stupid flash drive in it. I locked the box. I had forgotten why I had come into the room, and I headed into the hall. Jill pushed past me, and I almost tripped.

Why had I gone in there? I felt it was important.

Oh yeah, I needed a computer and a flash drive.

Flash drive!

There was one in the secret box.

I sat on Hillary's bed and opened the box, my hands trembling as I took out the flash drive and then slipped it into my pocket. I locked the box, hoping she wouldn't know it was gone until I could return it. Curiosity got the better of me, and I snooped through the other items on her shelf. She had a few pictures and some jewelry. I picked up a pile of bracelets.

"What are you doing, thief?" Hillary pointed her phone at me and snapped a picture.

My heart jumped out of my chest and hit the ceiling. I dropped the bracelets back on the shelf.

"You don't ever, ever, ever belong in my room. Is that clear?"

I jumped off her bed. Hillary looked like the rat at that moment, as if white bubbles foamed on her chin.

She grabbed my wrist and pulled at my bracelet from Marge.

"Give me my bracelet back," she said.

"This is mine."

"I very much doubt that. You stole it from me just now. I saw you."

"No. Marge, the counselor from school, gave it to me." I sounded like one of the babysat toddlers as I wailed.

"Why would the counselor give you a bracelet?"

"Because she likes me." I wouldn't tell Hillary that Marge had rescued me. I bet Hillary would have drunk the vodka if she had been with those kids.

"I very much doubt that." Hillary unclipped the bracelet from my wrist.

"Give it back!" I said, sounding even more like one of the toddlers. I didn't have a defense.

"You stole it from me."

"Marge is very special to me. Give it back!" I reached for the bracelet, but Hillary slapped my hand away. It left a red mark on my arm. "I am going to tell Peggy!"

Hillary held her phone up and showed me the picture she had taken of me holding all her bracelets.

"I'll just tell her it is mine, and you were here stealing my jewelry. I have evidence. Who will she believe?"

I had no defense. Besides, if I told Peggy that Marge had given it to me, Peggy would call Marge to verify the story and learn about Bear Lake. I wanted to bury that story forever.

Hillary pushed me across her room, and I stumbled to the ground. My hands went into a plate of something sticky and gross.

"You know the only reason my mom, not your mom, my mom is fostering you? Because she gets paid hundreds of dollars a month to do it. She doesn't care about you, just like she doesn't care about any of the kids she babysits. You are just like an extended babysitting job."

Hillary was such a jerk! I wiped my hand on her carpet to get the sticky off. Little pieces of carpet fuzz and dust cling to the sticky.

"I am keeping the bracelet as the entry fee for trespassing into my room. You will never come in here again, do you understand? -you stupid, annoying foster sister."

I stood up.

"If I ever find you in here again, I will beat you."

I ran out into the hall, and Hillary practically slammed the door on me. I looked at my bare wrist. I wanted my bracelet back. Hillary had no right to take it from me.

At least I found a flash drive I could use for my assignment. I felt a small amount of triumph, taking it from Hillary's secret box. If she is going to steal my things, then I would steal hers.

I just needed to find a computer.

Rhett let me use his computer, and I spent the rest of the night creating a PowerPoint for class. Surprisingly, Rhett took the time to show me how to add embellishments and animations. It looked pretty legit when I finished.

"Do you have something to save it on? You can't take my computer to school." He said as he shoved a candy bar into his mouth. I watched as little flakes of chocolate stuck to his bottom lip. I wanted to try a candy bar. I could smell its sweetness, and it looked amazing. Kids at school were always eating them, but no one ever shared a bite with me.

"I have a flash drive," I said, pulling it out of my pocket.

Rhett put it on the computer. "Your flash drive is almost full. You might want to go through it at some point and clear out all the files you no longer need."

"Sure, "I said, not knowing what he meant.

Rhett saved my PowerPoint presentation and then handed me the flash drive.

"Remember to talk slow. Look around the room when you talk. Try to memorize it. Smile, smile, smile."

So many instructions! I will never get this right.

Chapter 5

THE DAY FOR THE PRESENTATION came, and I didn't feel ready.

"And as you can see, we would all benefit from a little more kindness," Hillary said as she finished her PowerPoint. Everyone clapped.

What a fraud! She knows nothing of kindness.

"All right, Alora, How about you follow your sister."

The flash drive had gotten wet in my sweaty hands. I wiped it on my stupid dress. I hated dresses, but most of the time, it was the only thing I could find to wear in the laundry room, and usually, they were stained, wrinkled, smelly, and usually too short. I might actually look good for the presentation if I wore cute clothes. Alashia had been kind enough to do my hair in the morning when she heard I would be presenting.

Mrs. Palmer handed me the remote to the computer.

"You press here to go forward or here to go back. Now slip your flash drive in and begin when you are ready."

The flash drive opened on the computer screen, and I was confused by all the file names. My heart raced. What had Rhett saved it under? I felt all eyes bore into me while I searched the file names.

What did Rhett save it as?

One file said homework. That had to be it. All the other files had silly names.

I opened the file on the screen and turned to the class. Rhett's words played in my mind. "Don't stare at your presentation while you present. Remember to face the audience. Scan your eyes across their faces, but look at them, not the screen."

I tried to look at everyone's faces, but my eyes looked down to the floor.

Rhett's words continued in my head, "If that gets too hard, picture them naked. If nothing else, that will get you to laugh."

I tried to picture everyone naked, and I am sure my cheeks went red as a little giggle escaped me. "I am Alora Funk, and I chose The Value of Education to present on." Again, my eyes looked down to the ground.

The class gasped. I shouldn't have pictured them naked and giggled. I had to get serious.

I advanced the slide and tried to look up at the class. Their murmuring grew louder. I was failing at presenting. Rhett had made it sound way easier to present than it was.

"American children today do not understand the privilege they have," I said in almost a whisper as I clicked forward.

"Alora," the teacher said.

The remote shook in my hand. What did the teacher want? Did she want me to speak louder? I was surprised that the class wasn't looking at me but Hillary.

I clicked forward. "In 1852,"

"Alora, stop!" Hillary screamed.

What was she talking about?

I turned and looked at the screen behind me. There was a picture of Hillary and her friends spray painting the girl's locker room.

Oh my! This isn't my presentation. I am going to fail for sure. What if Rhett didn't actually save it?

I tried to find my file but ended up advancing the pictures. Another picture appeared of the girls in the school's kitchen. One person stood in a flour bin, one sat in a container of noodles, and Hillary dumped dirt in the rice bin.

Scandalous!

I hit forward on the remote and saw a picture of a kid going through the principal's file cabinet while Hillary stood on his desk.

A fist met my face and knocked me down. My eye ached as my head filled with flashing lights. That hurt terribly. Hillary ripped the remote out of my hand.

Mrs. Palmer ejected the flash drive.

"Give it to me," Hillary demanded of Mrs. Palmer. Hillary looked deranged, almost as if her eyes were spinning.

"Oh, I don't think so. In fact, you need to take a walk with me to the principal's office."

Hillary bent over me. "I will get you for this. I will get you so hard!" She kicked her foot into my ribs as she followed Mrs. Palmer out of the classroom.

It turned out that Hillary and her friends were the ones who had vandalized the school that the announcements kept talking about. It took me a bit to figure that out. They were suspended for the rest of the school year. They also had a real chance of receiving criminal charges.

"Here is the list of items to bring when you go to court," Peggy told Hillary on the day of her court trial. "You are lucky they didn't send you to youth jail. Your friend Lacey went to the detention center because she has a juvenile record."

"I don't have a record," Hillary said snottily, snapping her gum.

"You do now."

"You tarnished the Sanibel name," Mike growled as he played his video game.

"You mean the reputation of that hick family with way too many kids. I don't think there is a thing I can do that would tarnish our name. It is already crap in the community. We wear garbage thrift clothes, we drive a stupid nursing home bus, and we are filthy."

Mike threw the remote across the room. "Don't attack our family to clear your name." He suddenly seemed as big and ferocious as a grizzly bear. I ducked even though his anger wasn't at me.

Hillary didn't seem one bit scared. "I am not. Just stating the facts."

Peggy got in her face. "Watch yourself. You aren't allowed on any student government or club next year in middle school. Why did you do it?"

Hillary fingered the gum in her mouth and stretched it past her face. "It was fun," she said proudly.

"No remorse. That is sad. So sad. I hope the court slaps a huge fine and community service on you. Actually, I hope they sentence you to be locked in the detention center for a week. It would be good for you to learn a little humility. Speaking of humility, take out all the garbage." Mike picked up his remote and muttered something under his breath.

Hillary looked at her manicured nails. "As if."

"Fine, lose your phone," Peggy said, taking over.

Hillary stood up and glared at me, as she passed by, she whispered in my ear. "I know what I am going to do to get you back. It is good. It is classic. Good luck being able to live here after I ruin your name as you ruined mine."

Bits of her hate zipped through the air around me, crashing into my aura and filling me with fear.

⸺⬦⸺

I SAT ON THE CARPET with Alashia and played a board game. "Mike, get in here," Peggy yelled. Mike exited the bedroom and kicked over our game on his way to the couch.

"Dad, "Alashia whined.

"The floor ain't the place to play a game." Mike turned and kicked our pieces, scattering them everywhere. Mike faced Peggy. "What is it?" He seemed in a particularly sour mood as he growled his question.

"You remember Marge Humphrey?"

"Should I?"

Peggy made the voice of a witch, "Yes, you should."

Peggy waited, and then Mike barked. "Tell me or don't." He turned his body back toward his bedroom.

"Marge Humphrey is the counselor at ACYI. She really helped Corbon when he was going through that 'thing'. Plus, before she was married, Marge was Marge Spackman, and I ran for the student body with her in ninth grade."

"Good for her. Why should I care about her now?"

"When the news comes back on, they said they had details about a car robbery that involves her." Peggy clasped her hands together. "I hope nothing bad happened to her. She's a real solid gal."

Mike's voice elevated high, "She stole a car?"

"Welcome back," the anchor said. "Marge Humphrey, a beloved counselor at ACYI, discovered her car gone last night. Two hours later, the police found it in the neighboring town of Corrine. The car had been smashed into a tree. The police say they have strong leads."

"Can't trust anyone anymore. I think we should get one of those clubs they put on the steering wheel so no one steals our van." Mike said, sitting next to Peggy.

Alashia looked up. "No one is stealing our stupid van. If they did, that would be a blessing.

⎯⎯⎯◉⎯⎯⎯

THE MOMENT YOU TAKE the tests, you are no longer safe. Everyone will know what an idiot I am.

At least, that is what I thought.

I couldn't believe I would have to take another test. I felt a little comfort knowing all the other students were also testing.

"All right, students, remember, you will spend next week doing end-of-year testing in all your classes. Ensure you get plenty of sleep and eat a healthy breakfast." The announcements said just before releasing us for the weekend.

Before I knew it, the day of testing came, and I could hardly walk down the bus steps as my knees locked. I wanted to avoid taking the tests. At least all my teachers allowed me to take their master textbooks home since they knew I was at a disadvantage. Strangely, our classes didn't provide textbooks for us. Since I had missed most of the school year, the teachers wanted to give me access to the knowledge they had never taught me.

"Come play," Chrisitan begged me. "You have been studying those books for almost two weeks straight."

"I have to do good on the tests," I replied. His offer tempted me. Outside, the sun shone, and spring had transformed Mantua into a green wonderland. I loved outside more than being stuck in the stinky, chaotic Sanibel home.

"Those tests don't matter." He tossed a ball at my head, and it bounced off and rolled under the table.

"They do for me. The principal told Peggy..."

"Mom." Christian knew that Peggy had asked me to start calling her mom. I still couldn't do it.

"The principal said that since they didn't know where my learning baseline sat, the tests would help place me for next year's grade. If I do poorly, I might have to retake seventh grade. Or worse, go into sixth. I want to move on to middle school with my friends."

"I didn't think you had friends."

I covered my face with my hands. His words hurt. I had friends, didn't I? I think Rhonda was my friend.

Christian took my textbook and ran outside.

"Give me my book back," I wailed, chasing after him. When I got close, he threw the book into a pile of dirt and ran across the road. I picked up the book, and the edges were covered in mud. I tried to wipe it off, but it only smeared across the pages, staining them brown.

"Be very careful with this book," the teacher had told me.

"I will," I had promised.

Great. What would happen if I returned it in this condition?

I went back inside and continued scanning the books into my memory. It would be a long night.

As I walked into school on test day, I observed the other kids. They ran around with each other and carried on as they always did. They didn't harbor the same worry that I felt. I guess they didn't have the same weight of passing as I did. Regardless of how they did, they would all move up one grade next year. What if I was held back? My legs became stiffer.

We spent the day testing, and it surprised me how easy the tests were. I had ready access in my brain to every bit of information I had read. I could see the textbook pages clearly in my mind with real-time charts and images. I also had videos running if I needed them.

As I walked to the bus after school, my legs felt lighter, almost like I could fly.

I think I'll be advancing to middle school next year!

I wasn't prepared for what awaited me at school the next day.

We had just finished the science test, and Mrs. Jennings put a movie on as our reward. During an intense scene in the film, the office called me down.

They are going to make me miss the movie. What do they want now? I slapped the desk, and a few eyes looked at me.

I entered a large office and found Peggy and the principal waiting for me. This time, Dr. Schmidt didn't stand to greet me. Matching red auras illuminated from both of them. My bottom lip spasmed, and I covered it with my hand.

"Sit," Dr. Schmidt said in a low growl.

Now, my top lip joined the quivering. I sat at the far end of the table to put as much space between me and the tiny mob.

"I will get straight to the point. We had a breach of security on our computers. One of our trusted students accessed all the teacher's tests, made copies, and sold them to students at this school."

Peggy gave a pious gasp.

"Yes, I know," the principal responded. "It turns out that Alora has bought those tests."

I jumped out of my seat. "I did not!"

"Alora!" Peggy's voice came out scratchy and shrill. "How could you? Sanibels don't cheat. We never cheat. If you needed help studying, I would have been there for you. All you needed to do is ask."

Whatever!

"I did not cheat!"

"You took three tests yesterday and got a hundred percent on all three. That is quite the feat for someone who missed most of the school year. We have a couple of top ace students at this school, and they got in the low 90s. You did better than them, and I doubt that is possible."

My collar scratched and tightened my throat. I pulled at it. "I took every teacher's textbook home and have been studying. I did not cheat."

"Humph," Dr. Schmidt said, rubbing his chin.

"I DIDN'T!" I yelled. My hands covered my face. I had never used such an intense voice.

"Watch your tone, young lady," Peggy warned.

"Our teachers are going to have to spend the next two days rewriting the tests. That is asking a lot of them, especially when trying to finalize their grading books. We will retest on Thursday and Friday, which is too bad because those days were supposed to be spent doing end-of-school fun activities and assemblies. Now, the students will just have to test. By being so selfish, Alora, you have robbed the rest of the students of a fun tradition here at ACYI."

"I didn't cheat," I said in a more controlled voice. Tears ran down my cheeks.

"We have a zero-tolerance policy on cheating. We haven't decided what to do with you yet, but most likely, you will have to redo seventh grade." They expected me to admit to doing it. I could see it in their eyes.

"You can't do this to me." I groaned, standing to my feet, but my mind went swirly, and I had to sit.

Peggy glared at me. "That is just the start of your problems, young lady. Just wait for the punishment waiting at home for you."

"Test me right now!" I spoke. "Ask me anything, and I will answer it. Anything. Let me prove to you I didn't cheat." I hoped my head would stop spinning if they did.

"This is ridiculous," Dr. Schmidt said. He winced with disapproval and looked at Peggy for backup.

Nancy's voice came from the doorway. I hadn't realized she had been standing there. "5678950 divided by 99891."

"What are you doing? The principal barked at her as his chair squeaked from his sudden movement.

"Giving Alora a chance to prove herself."

"No one can answer that. Try something from her curriculum," Peggy said in her baby voice. I could never understand why she used it.

"This is ridiculous," Dr. Schmidt said again.

I closed my eyes. I loved how easily it had become to shift into my intellectual field. When I did, the numbers aligned in my mind effortlessly, and quickly the answer appeared. "56.8574681002. It keeps going, but I will stop there."

"What?" Dr. Schmidt said. His hands slapped the table, and we jolted from the sound.

"That was the answer. 56.8574681002. It keeps going."

Nancy pulled her phone out. "What was it again? 567...something divided by something. I can't remember what I said."

"You said 5678950 divided by 99891," I said slowly enough to give her time to calculate it. She looked up in amazement.

"Now, slowly repeat your answer."

"56.8574681002. It keeps going."

"Do that again," she challenged. "How about 951159 divided by 753357?"

The equation lined up, and I saw all the steps in solving it. "1.262560, and this number keeps going." I was so fast that Nancy hadn't punched all the numbers yet. When she did, she blankly stared at me.

"Give her something hard," Principal Schmidt said.

Did he really say that? I bet he couldn't solve that equation in his head. He probably couldn't even crack it without a pencil and paper. He left his office and came back with a paper. "Here is a problem in one of my puzzles. A=PI*r2 if A=113.04sq ft and PI*=3.14, what is r?"

Nancy leaned over his shoulder and looked at the problem. "That isn't seventh-grade math."

"No kidding," Peggy replied.

The equation lined up in front of me, solving itself. When it was done, the answer was clear. "r=6," I said.

"Get me a scrap paper and a pencil," Principal Schmidt said.

Nancy left and came back with a piece of paper and a pencil. Dr. Schmidt worked through the problem. "Hah! You are wrong. The answer is not 6; it is 23."

"Then you did it wrong," I said with confidence. "It is 6 and nothing else."

Principal Schmidt reworked the problem. Then his head popped up. "Oops, I was wrong. The answer is 12."

"No, it is 6 and nothing else."

Principal Schmidt looked down at the paper. He had already used both sides. Just then, Marcus Skinner walked by, the sixth-grade math teacher.

"Hey Marcus, get in here and solve this," he said.

Skinner sat and scribbled a few things down. "I need a scientific calculator," he said. Principal Schmidt ducked out of the room and then returned with a calculator. Skinner worked on the problem. "r=6," he said.

"Are you sure?" Principal Schmidt asked.

"Yup," Skinner said as he was leaving the room. "Sorry, I need to get back to class."

Peggy watched in astonishment, and so did Nancy. I wanted to jump on the table and dance over their faces.

"I tell you, I didn't cheat," I said. "Let's just say I am getting some of my memory back."

"She has me convinced," Nancy smiled at me. She had always been nice to me from the first time that I had met her.

"Listen," Principal Schmidt said with a beet-red face. His aura turned teal. He must have felt stupid getting bested by the 'dumb seventh grader'.

"You will retake your tests in the office on Thursday and Friday under direct supervision. If you get caught cheating, then you will redo seventh grade next year."

Peggy stood up. "I have to get going." She looked at her watch. "Important things to get done."

Like watching all those babysat kids!

Peggy didn't even look at me as she left the room.

My tongue turned into a thick wad in my mouth. I had to say it as I left. "I didn't cheat!"

⸻ ◉ ⸻

DING. DONG.

"Alora, the door for you," Hillary said, personally delivering the message. She had a smug look that I didn't trust and a mustard-yellow aura that I didn't like. I had never seen anyone with such an ugly aura before. I went to the entryway and saw two cops.

She is just messing with me.

I turned to walk away, but Hillary blocked me. "Seriously, Alora. I ain't messing around. They are here for you."

"Are you Jane Doe?" the police asked. I shifted on my feet and then forced myself to stop.

Maybe this had something to do with them capturing the Russians. I relaxed. That would be good news. Now I would know who I was.

"Yes,"

"We need you to come to the station for questioning."

"Mom, Dad," Hillary screamed right in my ear. -such a Sanibel thing to do. My ear throbbed.

Mike appeared. When he saw the police, he stood taller and tucked his wife-beater tank top into his shorts.

"Something wrong?" he asked.

"Yes, we need you to bring Jane Doe to the station for questioning."

"When?"

"Now." The cops didn't seem like they were delivering good news. They seemed pissed. Shouldn't they be there for Hillary, not me?

"Let me grab my keys, and I will follow behind you."

The heavy silence at the police station felt like thick tar had been poured on us while the vast space in the nursing home van seemed to swallow me up.

What have they found? Maybe the police know who my parents are, and I will never have to return to the Sanibel home again! It's not that I didn't like it at the Sanibels. It's just that I didn't love it either. I wanted to find my family, one that cared for me and didn't take me in just to make foster money.

"Mr. Sanibel. Jane. We both need your statement of what Jane did Saturday night."

"What?" What did that have to do with telling me who my family was?

Mike seemed confused as well. "What does this have to do with?"

People hustled around us in the police station. I had seen a police TV show once, but this seemed different.

"Make your statements, then we will tell you."

The police separated us, and I kept popping my knuckles as I tried to remember what I had done. What did I do Saturday night? Every night was the same at the Sanibel's. I remembered turning Peggy down to go to the reservoir, and I stayed in my room and studied.

"I spent the day and night studying," I wrote. They told me I had to sign it with my legal name, Jane Doe. That was not my legal name. It was only the crappy one they assigned to me. The police brought Mike and me back together.

"What is this all about?" Mike asked, rubbing his elbows. White flakes of skin fell onto his basketball shorts.

"We have reason to believe that Jane Doe stole Marge Humphry's car Saturday night and crashed it into a tree."

"What!" Out of all the things I imagined being brought to the police station for, this idea was preposterous.

"I don't even know how to drive."

"That was obvious with everything the car hit before it crashed."

"I don't know where Marge lives. I don't know where Corrine is. There is no way, and I mean no way I could have done that." I felt sparks of anger and hate fly off me. I wanted to take the pile of papers on the cop's desk and throw them across the room. I knew that wouldn't help my cause, so I just stuffed my arms behind my back.

"How did you know it crashed in Corrine? We didn't tell you that part of the case." Both cops got closer and folded their arms.

How did I know?

"We watched it on the news," Mike said, saving me.

The cop put a safe on the desk and then opened it. He pulled a bracelet out and put it on a square of material. "Do you recognize this bracelet?" He asked.

Mercy me! It was the bracelet Marge had given me. What were the cops doing with it?

"How about you try it on?" the police said.

"Don't!" Mike yelled.

Everyone jumped and looked at him.

"Don't let them trick you and get your fingerprints on it."

"We have a statement from Marge Humphreys stating she knows that the bracelet left at the crime scene was the one she had given you. She is prepared to file charges to the full extent of the law."

My heart turned inside out. Marge was my only true friend, or so I thought. The cop's words kicked me in the gut. How could Marge do this to me? The cop pulled a strand of golden hair out of the safe and held it to mine.

"Looks like an exact match to me," he said. He took out some scissors and snipped a bit of my hair off. "We will send both of them to the lab to run a DNA match on them."

Mike put his body in between the cops and mine. "You had no right to cut her hair. We are done here. If you want more information, you can talk to our public defender. We are done here." Mike grabbed my hand and led me out of the police station. Suddenly, and strangely, Mike was my new hero.

What a week! The first of it, I was accused of cheating. The middle of it, I was accused of stealing a car. What next?

At school, I was forced to test in a room behind the office while supervised. Originally, Marge was supposed to sit with me, but she refused. She went out of her way to avoid me. A couple of times, she saw me, then ducked into her office. Her rejections felt like she had an ice pick, and she was puncturing my heart with it, filling it full of a million little holes.

Thankfully, the only thing that went right that week was that I scored perfect on all tests, and this time, no one could accuse me of cheating.

Chapter 6

HILLARY AND I BOTH awaited our court dates, which both happened to be June 17. Mine was for stealing Marge's car, joyriding, and property damage. Hillary's was for vandalizing and trespassing the school.

I had no way to prove my innocence. I didn't have an alibi for the night the car was stolen. I knew Hillary was behind the car robbery and crash. She had planted my things in Marge's car to frame me. Why had she done that? The real question was, did she steal the car, joyride, and then crash, or did she steal the car with the intention to crash and frame me?

After my PowerPoint presentation, when she and her friends were caught, she treated me twenty times worse than she had before.

"If you hadn't stolen my flash drive, none of this would have ever happened." She continuously told me.

"Peggy told me to look for a flash drive in your room."

"Yeah, but she didn't tell you to break into my private box. If you had minded your business, we wouldn't have been caught. It is all your fault."

If you hadn't committed the crime, you wouldn't have gotten caught.

"You will pay hard for this."

And I was. She framed me for a serious crime. She destroyed my friendship with Marge. Marge hated me.

ON A RARE SATURDAY morning, I woke up to find the house to myself. Everyone seemed to be at soccer games or doing their own thing outside the home. As I made my way down the stairs, I tripped on a shoe, somersaulted down two, and hit the floor with a loud crash.

Instantly, the most horrific pain shot through my arm. My ulna bone poked through my right arm. Blood smeared everywhere, and the pain moved into every part of me.

"Ahhhhh," I screamed so loud that the force sheared my throat.

"I want to die. I want to die," I screamed.

As I rolled around the floor in pain, I saw a video in my head of a surgeon pinning a shattered ulna bone together. Could I do that? I tried to concentrate on the molecules in my arm but stopped when another bout of pain rippled through me. My breaths came out short and heavy as my shirt soaked in sweat.

I tried again.

I imagined the bone realigning, then the molecules fusing the break back together. As I did, tremendous pain almost made me pass out until I noticed I couldn't see the bone through the skin anymore and that the arm no longer looked crooked.

I had done it! I had fixed my bone. I thought about the nerves and veins by the ulna and imagined them healing and the skin closing up without a mark. Again, to my astonishment, it did.

I ran my left hand over my right arm, and everything felt whole, but the throbbing and aching intensified. I then shut off the axons from spreading the message that I hurt. Instantly, the pain was gone. I looked at my healed arm and cried.

I had done it! I had healed myself.

Despite the filth of the carpet, I sprawled out on the ground and let feelings of euphoria overcome me. I had powers to control and fix man! No wonder the Russians had feared me.

After about twenty minutes of doing nothing, I noticed the dry blood on my clothes and carpet. I used my mind to release the molecules, and the stains disappeared. Maybe it was time to use these same forces and clean the filthy home I lived in.

I used my mind to pick up all the trash, which I put in a giant pile in the kitchen. Then, I sent all the toys, clothes, and scattered junk flying back to their respective storage spots. I removed stains from the walls, carpet, and couch. By the time two hours had passed, I had made the house cleaner than it had probably looked in forty years.

I studied the massive pile of garbage in the kitchen, deciding what to do with it when I remembered the theories of rearranging molecules and turning things into something else. I transformed all the molecules in the trash and created food. I could hardly believe it worked. Even though I had healed my arm, turning molecules into other things amazed me. I lined the three tables with a grand feast.

There was turkey, burgers, squash, potatoes, stuffing, cakes, pies, rolls, sushi, and so much more incredible food. As I sat down to eat, the first of the Sanibels returned home.

I heard Mike, Joshua, and Elizabeth walk through the entryway.

"What! What! What!" Mike sounded like a football player calling out plays on the field.

"Daddy!" Elizabeth squeaked.

"Whose been in our house?" Joshua squealed. He reminded me of the baby bear after discovering Goldy Locks.

The three of them ran into the room with the tables and saw me sitting before the feast.

"How did this house get so clean?" Mike demanded, throwing his hands on his hips. As his wrist bent backward, he looked like a deranged chicken.

Joshua and Elizabeth stopped asking questions and dove into the food on the table. Mike bent over, grabbed a giant turkey leg, and came to my side.

"Who did this? Was this the church? I am embarrassed. They had no right to come into my house," he snarled as he ripped a strip of meat off the bone. Greasy juice dribbled down his chin and landed at the collar of his yellowed wife-beater tank top.

I heard the front door open and could hear Peggy's incessant chatter come into the house, and then it stopped.

"Mike, what is going on?"

The table shook as she ran into the room. Nina, Christian, and a few neighbor kids were by her side. All the kids did the same thing. Without a word, they dove into the feast. Elizabeth was already halfway through a pie when the others joined her. She ridged her back and snarled. Those Sanibels acted like a pack of angry dogs.

Peggy ignored the food and left to explore the rest of the house. I could hear her gasp in amazement as she went around and noticed how clean everything was. She even went upstairs. Eventually, she returned to where we were. As she popped a sushi in her mouth, she asked, "Who did all this? It was like a fairy visited our house while we were gone."

Nina smiled with her toothless grin. "I did have a birthday yesterday. This was my wish."

Peggy popped another sushi in her mouth. "You wished for a clean house and feast," she said through a mouth stuffed with food. Little pieces of rice flew out of her mouth as she spoke.

"Well, no. I wished for a doll. But this is probably for my birthday from the fairies."

"I think Alora did this," Joshua said, pointing a spoon filled with mashed potatoes at me.

Before I could answer, Peggy said, "She couldn't have. She was with me the whole time."

I sat straight up. "Seriously," I said out loud, but no one seemed to hear me.

"Then who did it?" Joshua asked.

Mike reached across the table and grabbed a burger. "The church did it, that is who. They had no right to come into our house without permission."

"How dare they," Peggy agreed, cramming a roll into her mouth.

The lot of them made me sick as they shoved so much food in their mouth without even taking a breath.

"It was me," I said, but my words were drowned out by more voices coming in the front door. Corbon, Rhett, and Hillary entered the room with the tables.

"What is going on?" Hillary demanded, then dove for the table, followed by her brothers.

I stopped trying to tell them it was me. No one listened or believed me anyway; besides, I liked how mad they got when they thought the church had come in and done it.

⸺⬤⸺

BRIGHAM CITY HOSTED a movie in the park, and we dragged blankets, sleeping bags, pillows, and treats to the park. As all the kids and friends spread out, the Sanibel section took up a third of the grassy area. It was the most fun night I had there. I loved the energy of the crowd and all the people running around.

Christian, Alashia, and I wandered around the baseball field as we waited for the movie to start. My stomach had been hurting quite a bit, but I was having too much fun to think about healing myself.

"There is the girl that ruined our lives," Hillary said. I looked up as she and her groupies surrounded me. I grabbed Christian's hand as if he could protect me against the five-bloodthirsty mob. Rhonda glared at me. When did she turn on me? Having Rhonda on Hillary's side was almost as painful as losing Marge's friendship.

"There is the girl responsible for ruining our lives," Hillary said.

Even though she didn't touch me, it felt like Hillary repeatedly kicked me in the gut. I collapsed in pain and grasped my stomach.

"Stop faking it," Hillary said.

No one could fake that intense pain. I couldn't help screaming as I rolled into the fetal position and passed out.

⸺⬤⸺

A SCREAM CAME FROM the room next door, and I shuddered. There I was, back in the hospital. The place of my earliest memory. I looked at the bandage covering my lower belly.

It turns out my appendix had burst, and I was taken by ambulance to the hospital. I would wake up a few times, but I couldn't heal myself because I didn't know what was wrong with me. I thought maybe I had eaten bad food, but as I tried to fix my stomach, there was nothing to fix. I hadn't even thought about my appendix.

I didn't know what the doctors planned to do when they put me under anesthesia.

"We want you to take some deep breaths into this mask," they had said.

"Are you trying to put me under?" Fear fluttered inside me. If they told me what was wrong, I could fix myself. But they didn't.

"Oh no, this is just oxygen. Your oxygen saturation is low."

I believed them. I took six breaths, and that was it.

I was under.

Peggy came into the hospital room as someone screamed again.

"The doctor said you can go home tomorrow," she said.

"What day is tomorrow?"

"It is June 17th."

I tried to sit up, but the tightness in my abdomen kept me down.

"I have court tomorrow. Are they going to make me go? Maybe I can get discharged on the 18th so that I will miss court."

"Oh, you didn't hear?" Peggy said.

"Hear what."

"The charges have been dropped against you."

A relief sweeter than the peach ice cream I had eaten at the movie night overcame me.

"Why did they drop the charges?"

"After you were taken to the hospital. Rhonda and all of Hillary's friends felt bad for you. They thought they had caused your emergency.

So, Rhonda went and told her mom about their revenge plot against you. They had purposely stolen and crashed Marge's car, then framed you for it."

Peggy's words stung and yet balmed simultaneously. I knew they had a plot. To have Peggy say it out loud validated my thoughts.

"Rhonda's mom took her to the police station, where she confessed to stealing Marge's car and framing you for it."

"I knew it!" I yelled, then gripped my stomach.

"They arrested Hillary and her friends, and they will remain in detention at least until tomorrow. I think it will be longer since the court date for tomorrow is only for the charges against the school. Their joyriding charges and vehicle theft have yet to be charged."

I felt amazing to no longer have criminal charges against me. I felt terrible that Rhonda was arrested, but I was relieved to have my name cleared.

"Oh, this is for you," Peggy said. She pointed to a large bouquet of mylar balloons and a box of chocolates.

"You can have the chocolate after you recover, but here is the card."

I opened the envelope and saw a card with a butterfly on the front. "Dear Alora,

I owe you a thousand apologies. I am sorry for my cruel and unkind behavior toward you. I believed you had stolen my car, and I felt such betrayal from you. As it turns out, you had nothing to do with it, and it was I who betrayed you."

Marge's words filled the inside and back of the card. She ended by reminding me I could go to her for anything. I liked the apology but didn't know how to overcome the extreme pain she had caused me.

Having my name cleared did wonders for my morale. I felt such relief. However, something even more significant happened. Apparently, my body recognized the anesthesia they had given me for surgery. Perhaps it was the same drug the Russians had used on me in their basement. It seemed to regenerate the pathways in my mind and unlock my brain's barrier. My intellectual thinking exploded, and I could not shut it off. Suddenly, I analyzed everything. My quest for knowledge drove me mad. I would often have Mike drop me off at the library on his way to work, and I would take in as many books each day as possible. All I had to do was scan over the page, and everything not only stayed with me, but it would often open a cache of information I seemed to know already. I became addicted to knowledge, and books were my drug.

The anesthesia was supposed to have made me unconscious, and from my outside appearance, everyone thought I was. But my mind was aware of everything that went on during surgery. It made me hyper-aware.

I felt every slice of their surgical knife, with the pain like a giant vice grip, gripping tighter and tighter, sharper and stronger. I wanted to scream out in the most horrific pain but couldn't move.

My body recognized the drugs they pumped through my IV. I can't explain the reaction my brain and blood cells had. It was like a family reunion, my body rejoicing to be under the influence of the chemicals again.

Soon, my mind went on a psychedelic trip. I saw colors not seen in real life. Math equations and scientific formulas zoomed forward, solving quicker than a computer could.

Knowledge and facts flooded me. Definitions and maps filled my head. If I wasn't under the supervision of the hospital, I would have thought I was on an acid trip or something.

It was crazy that the pain of the surgery and the mind trip all happened together, like a million stimulants all at once.

———◦———

ON JUNE 23, I FELL out of love for my Sandibel family.
Ding Dong.

"Jane!" Rhett called from the door. I looked up. Christian and I had spent the morning in a drawing game, even though I would have rather been at the library. Why had Rhett called me Jane? "I'll be back, "I told Christian. I had to force myself to walk to the door. The last time someone had come for me, it had been the cops.

Dr. Schmidt and a strange man stood in the entryway among our pile of shoes. After cleaning the house, it took only a short time for the Sanibels had it trashed again. I think there were more shoes in the entryway than you could find at the shoe store. Seeing my principal made my heart race. I wiped my clammy hands on the side of my dress.

Why is he here asking for me? After he accused me of cheating, I disliked him.

"Jane, this is Mr. Ludwig Van Hassel." A distinguished-looking man stood by Dr. Schmidt.

"Good afternoon, Jane." I instantly knew he was entirely of German descent, yet he lacked an accent.

Dr. Schmidt continued, "He is in charge of a prestigious science camp at Harvard University. May we come in so Mr. Van Hassel can tell you about it?"

"Sure," I said. I turned toward the direction of the living room, and they followed. We walked through a path littered with garbage, papers, and dirty dishes. The smell of rotten fish marinating in fermented milk greeted us. What slobs my family were. What must this Harvard elite think of me?

Peggy sat on her chair watching soaps. She looked up.

"Oh, to what pleasure do we have of a house call from the principal in the summer?" She asked in a voice that sounded like a cartoon character.

"Peggy, this is Mr. Van Hassel from Harvard." Dr. Schmidt said.

"Thank you. I am actually Dr. Van Hassel."

"Sorry about that," Principal Schmidt said sheepishly. "This is *Doctor* Van Hassel."

I liked watching someone make Dr. Schmidt the fool.

"Speaking of names," I meekly interjected. "My name is Alora Funk." I bit on my thumb's nubby nail. I hated it when people called me Jane. It made my muscles tighten and burn.

"What?" Dr. Van Hassel asked, looking confused.

"Oh yes, we do need to get her name officially changed on the records," Principal Schmidt said. Did the principal agree on something with me?

"What did the professor say when the Urology student did not know the technical name for pee?" Peggy chimed in.

The two men turned to her. Their jaws dropped at her rude intrusion of such nonsense words.

"Urine, idiot." They stared at her as if fifty worms were crawling from her nose. This time, even Peggy didn't laugh at her joke.

"May we sit?" Dr. Schmidt asked. Where would they sit? The couch had clothes strung all over it.

Peggy answered, "I don't care." She didn't do anything to clear a spot for them. They both stiffened as they sat at the edge of the couch.

Dr. Van Hassel cleared his throat. "Alora, your curiosity must be bidding at you to discern why I sit in your living room. The truth of the matter is I have flown all the way here from Boston to introduce a highly coveted program offered by Harvard. -our prestigious science-focused summer camp. Kids your age apply almost a year in advance in hopes of procuring a spot. The camp starts on July 6 and goes on until August 5. We receive nearly a thousand applicants, but we only allow twenty kids into the program. DON'T TAKE MY WORDS LIGHTLY when I tell you it is a distinguished opportunity. We start the camp for seventh graders entering eighth grade. If you keep up on your work and receive high merit, we invite you back to defend your spot for the sequential years until your high school career ends. Alora, I must stress that having this camp on your resume gives you a twenty-three percent higher chance at being accepted into Harvard to start your university sophomore year."

What is he going on about?

"Don't you understand what I am saying?" he asked.

"Maybe," I said. Peggy made some sort of snorting sound as she focused on the TV. The professor gave her a look of pure disgust. I didn't blame him. His face reflected what I often thought about her.

"We are prepared to offer you a spot at this camp." He turned back to me. I tried to look prestigious as if I wasn't living with the Sanibels, but his words hit me.

"What? Why?" I stumbled over my reply. I had spent most of my time being told what a stupid, dumb girl I was.

"Marge Humphry is my niece," Dr. Van Hassel said.

I looked at him in confusion.

"Ms. Marge, the guidance counselor," Principal Schmidt clarified.

Hearing her name blasted mixed emotions in me. She had been my savior at Bear Lake. For that, I would always hold her in high regard. Yet, she had turned on me so quickly, souring the kindness I had felt for her. "Oh," was all I could say.

"When Marge disclosed the details of your story and academics, she piqued my interest. Such progress you made from your entrance into her school. Marge has never been one to exaggerate or glorify a situation."

I wouldn't be too sure about that.

"If she attested you scored perfectly on those tests, I have no reason to doubt her. She also told me about your little math game in the office. I realized the extent of your brilliance. I flew here to personally offer you a spot at our camp if you can pass a few tests of ours first."

Blah, more tests.

"Are you willing to do this?" he asked me as he stared intently into my eyes. I think he was trying to look at my brain. He wore a full beard, trimmed short and neat. He looked out of place in our hick home. Despite the summer heat, Dr. Van Hassel wore a full-blue suit with a vest underneath. No one at church even dressed that fine. I bet the Sanibels never had someone so classy in their home before. It probably killed Dr. Van Hassel to be amidst their garbage as he sat on their lumpy, springy couch. Why couldn't he have shown up the day I cleaned it?

And I sat at our introduction in the too-short summer dress, which I despised. I couldn't remember the last time it was washed. I felt aware of my inferiority and wanted to hide. Maybe after he saw what a slob our family was, he would change his mind.

"Are you?" he asked again.

I snapped my head up. "Yes," I said, not fully understanding the magnitude of his offer. The biggest thing I heard was I would get a breather from the Sanibel house. Spending the summer with them drove me crazy. School had given me a break from the filth and chaos of their home. I needed an out, and Harvard offered me that.

"You will go to the Utah State University Extension Campus in Brigham City. A procter will give you a series of tests. If you get an average of ninety-eight percent or better, then you have a spot at our camp. Your appointment is for 10 a.m. on Monday."

"Okay," I said. I looked at Peggy to see what she thought. She twisted her shirt collar as she focused on her soap opera, not hearing a word of our conversation. The TV's sound was off, but she mouthed the words from the closed captions.

"Before wasting anyone's time, I have a few equations for you to solve. Think of it as a pretest." Dr. Van Hassel said.

My heart sped up and bounded against my chest.

He pulled a sheet of paper out of his bag and put it in front of me. "Let me find you a pencil," he said, reaching back into his bag.

I looked at the equation on his paper. Before he pulled out the pencil, the equation set itself up in my mind, and it was solved. "x= 5". I spoke.

Dr. Van Hassel's head popped up, and his eyes bulged out. Instead of grabbing his pencil, he took a paper packet and put it in front of me. "There are three pages there, and they are all part of one equation," he said.

I flipped through the pages, my mind aligning and arranging things as it solved the problem. My abilities still astounded me.

How do I know this? Who was I before the hospital?

"54 liters," I said.

"Brilliant, brilliant," Dr. Van Hassel said." Lightning speed. Even quicker than my skills." He already had another sheet of paper in his hand. I took it from him. It wasn't a mathematical equation; it was a scientific question. I read it.

"Well," I said. "The answers are methylation, phosphorylation, and acetylation." How did I have such retention of knowledge? I couldn't explain. Had I known all this before my memory swipe? Maybe I was a secret CIA agent, and they had extracted my memory so I wouldn't compromise the agency. As of late, my mind seemed to recall many things. -just not memories.

A baby crawled into the living room. The odor from its diaper dominated the senses. Dr. Van Hassel put his thumb under his nose and then removed it. He struggled to keep a poker face as I saw his eyes crinkle. I wished Peggy would take care of the smell, but why would she? She didn't ever move from her spot watching TV during the day.

Dr. Van Hassel zipped his bag closed. "I am glad we did this. I can now see sending you to the campus on Monday to test would have only wasted everyone's time."

"Did I not pass?" I asked disappointedly, chewing harder on my nails.

How did I not pass? I knew the answers were correct. I wanted an escape from the Sanibels for the rest of the summer. Regret filled me with my lost opportunity.

"Oh, you more than passed. You blew the tests away. I want you to be at the airport Sunday night of July 5."

"Um, how much will it cost?" I asked. I hardly doubted the Sanibels could afford a plane ticket, let alone the price of camp.

"You are going to Harvard, Ms. Alora Funk. The camp alone is fifteen thousand dollars."

I gasped out loud. I wouldn't be attending. The Sanibels couldn't afford it, and they wouldn't spend that much on me even if they could.

Dr. Van Hassel gazed around the house in disgust. "I will find a scholarship for you to pay your expenses one hundred percent."

I wanted to jump up and down and run around the room excitedly but thought that might scare the doctor away, so I didn't react.

"Can you get her to the airport Sunday night, early Monday morning for a red-eye flight?" Dr. Van Hassel asked Peggy.

She looked up, "Huh? Are you talking to me?"

"Did you fail to pay attention to our conversation?" he asked disdainfully.

"Sorry, I didn't know you were here to talk to me."

"Mrs. Sanibel," Principal Schmidt said. "Dr. Van Hassel is from Harvard. He has flown all the way out here to offer Alora a spot at their very prestigious summer camp."

"We can't afford that," Peggy grumbled.

"He will be taking her there on a scholarship."

"I am not sure this is the right time in her life for something like this," Peggy said.

Her words rammed me in the gut. What was she talking about? Was she not going to let me go? I hadn't even considered she would want to stop me. Why?

"She has been through a lot and is finding stability in her life. That camp with hoity-toity people would put undue pressure on her and unravel all of our hard work."

What hard work could Peggy possibly be talking about? She hadn't even noticed when I stayed away for a night.

"Mrs. Sanibel, I don't think you realize what an opportunity this is for Alora. This is a fifteen thousand dollar full-ride scholarship we are offering. You won't pay a thing. There are close to a thousand kids who apply for this camp and will never get a chance to go. This program will build a foundation she cannot glean in a small town like this. Going to this camp might be her ticket into Harvard as a graduate student."

I could tell Peggy didn't like him insulting her town. "Maybe next year, boys," she said childishly.

What is she doing?

Who was she to block a lifetime opportunity for me? She wasn't my mom. Kids at school told me she was only fostering me for the monthly money they gave her. Now, she would prevent me from the greatest opportunity of my life!

"I have already bought her airline ticket," Dr. Van Hassel pushed on. He seemed like the type of guy that didn't take no. Finally, someone in my life fighting for me!

"Then that was a foolish move on your part," she tartly replied.

I am not a violent person, but at the moment, I wanted to hit her.

"Gentlemen, please see yourself out," she said as she turned the volume on the TV.

The men got up and went outside. I trailed behind them, unable to stop the tears pouring from my eyes.

"Change her mind," Dr. Van Hassel said to me. "I will keep your ticket and spot open." He handed me his business card, and the two drove away in a black limousine. All the neighborhood kids had gathered to see who rode around in such an automobile and why they had gone to the Sanibels'.

I saw my future drive away with them. I stood on dry, yellow grass. Most of the yard had died or gone to weeds. My chance was gone. Peggy was extremely stubborn. She wouldn't change her mind.

Why did she say no? What is it to her?

As I returned to the house, I slammed the door behind me. I stomped down the hall, through the dining room, and into the family room, planting myself in front of Peggy so she couldn't see the TV.

"Why can't I go?" I hissed. I put my hands on my hips like she often did.

"Calm down, Alora. Not everything is what it seems. I don't feel right about this, and I must listen to my gut."

"I don't care how you feel. This is my life, not yours, and I am going!" I yelled. I shook, for I had never been so brazen with her before.

"Don't you use that tone of voice with me," she said, elevating her own tone. "While you live under my roof, I am your mother, and I set your rules. Like it or not, that is how it works."

"But this is my life, not yours!"

"And I want to protect that life."

"You mean stifle it."

"Do you honestly think you can change my mind by yelling at me? That is not how it works; in fact, it is causing me to build the highest wall around this subject, a wall that will never be removed."

"How can you be so heartless?" I challenged.

"Go to your room!"

"Gladly," I said. I stomped up the stairs and slammed my door closed. I threw myself on my bed and bawled.

Out of all the foster homes in the area, why was I sent here?

I THOUGHT MIKE WOULD be on my team. How mistaken I was.

"And she won't let me go," I said as I finished my plea to Mike.

"Wow, don't get me involved. You are her project, not mine."

"Project," I roared. "I am not a project. I am a human."

"Whatever," he said as he chugged his soda.

As I headed to my room, I walked past it and ended up in Hillary's room. She shared it with Emma, Elizabeth, and Alashia. They were gone to soccer or something. I saw her special locked box smashed in pieces. She wanted to blame me for getting in trouble and not taking responsibility for committing the crime. Despite her beauty, she had to have a dark soul to frame me for her horrendous crime against Marge.

I once thought that Hillary and I would be friends, but it was apparent that would never happen. When she returned home from her stay in detention, she was even more nasty to me. I put my hand on the mattress to help push me up when I felt her phone. I pulled it out from the covers. It was dead, but her charger was on the shelf. I used my energy to power her phone to life, but I still couldn't use it without a password.

Could it be the same number that she used in her box? There is no way it could be that easy, could it? I put 2020 in, and the phone presented all the functions.

I dialed the number I had seen on much of my paperwork.

"Hello, Mr. Cox, Child and Family Services."

My voice came out soft and almost inaudible. "Um, yes, this is Alora Funk?"

"Who?"

"I am sorry. I mean Jane Doe." I wished that Child and Family Services would legally change my name.

"A surprise to hear you call me. What can I do for you?"

"The principal brought a guy over yesterday named Dr. Van Hassel. The professor offered me a full-ride scholarship to attend a prestigious summer school. He said it was a foot in the door for future placement in Harvard."

"We can arrange that for you."

"The problem is Peggy refuses to let me go. Can she do that?"

"Yes."

"Well, I want his offer. I want to go to Harvard for summer camp. How can I make this happen?"

"Is there any way you can change Peggy's mind?"

"I don't think so."

"Well, then we have one other option. We can give her a chance to let you go or terminate the placement."

"You mean they wouldn't be my foster parents anymore?"

"Correct."

"That seems extreme."

"I guess it depends on how important this camp is to you. Honestly, there are far superior foster homes than that one. The Sanibels were never my first pick. When you were released from the hospital, there weren't many options for you. Currently, we have twelve families trained and ready to take in a foster child. Any of those twelve would be better than the Sanibels."

The Sanibels were all I knew. Yes, I didn't love it there. I wished I had nice clothes that fit me when I went to school. I wished I had more food. I hoped that I had a dad that engaged with the family. I wished that half the neighborhood didn't always hang out there. I wished for many things but loved the reservoir across the street. I loved my special time with Peggy. I loved Marge, but I guess she had ruined that.

As we talked, I saw a crumpled piece of paper on Hillary's shelf.

"Die Alora," it said.

Never mind. It was time to leave.

Chapter 7

"OKAY. LET'S DO IT THAT way," I said.

"Are you asking to be placed in a new family if they refuse to allow you to go to Harvard?"

"Yes."

Silence.

"One um...one other thing. Can we change my name legally back to Alora Funk?"

"What do you mean back to?"

"Well, it's my real name."

"And how do you know that?"

"It is one of my few memories that have returned. I have no doubt that is my name."

I had lots of doubts it was my name. In all truthfulness, I probably made it up, but I wasn't going to tell Mr. Cox that.

"I will look into that."

"Thank you."

"One other thing. It is good to hear you have a voice."

Good thing he couldn't see me blush. "Thank you."

My opinion of Mr. Cox changed. I had feared him up to that day. Now, he almost felt like he was going to champion me on.

The following day, Mr. Cox showed up early. He caught Mike before he left for work.

"Perfect. I wanted to talk to both of you." Mr. Cox said when I brought Mike to him.

"Ugh, I don't know why?" Mike said, staring at his watch. "This isn't my project. Keep it quick. I have to get to work."

"Quick is how I like it. Where is your wife?"

"Peggy," Mike bellowed without shoving his face in anyone's ear.

"I watching the morning news," I heard a muffled reply.

"It must be important. CPS is here."

After a few minutes, Peggy joined us. She held a dirty diaper in her hand. She tossed it in the corner of the entryway, then wiped her hand on the side of her pants before reaching out to Mr. Cox.

"I am good," he said as his eyes stared at the filthy hand.

"Mr. Cock, so good of you to return," Peggy said, using her bubbly high cartoon voice. "What can we do for you, or have you come to do for us?"

"We are aware of the opportunity Jane has for a summer camp in Harvard."

Dang, he still called me Jane.

"She has let me know her intentions to go, and as child advocates, we want to ensure she gets that chance."

Peggy's face went red. "How do you know about this?"

"Jane called me."

Peggy looked like she wanted to backhand me across the face.

"Well, I don't feel good about it, and I have learned to trust my intuition. So, the answer is no. Thank you for coming out here." Peggy turned around.

"Peggy, I am afraid if you don't allow Jane to go, I will have to terminate her placement here."

"Because I am making a carefully thought decision to protect Alora, you are going to terminate Jane's placement here? I don't understand that. My cousin was in the foster system and got beat daily by this witch named Salina. Despite all the phone calls we made, they never removed my cousin from her foster mom." Peggy's voice choked. "Eventually, my cousin died by Salina's own hands. So, you guys don't terminate Salina for beating a kid, but you will terminate me for protecting a kid?"

"Peggy, Jane has made it clear that she wants the placement terminated if you refuse to let her go. This is about Jane and what Jane wants."

Peggy held her right fist, again looking like she was stopping herself from hitting me with it.

"Well, if you want out of here that bad, then go," Peggy said, walking away. "Don't let me get in the way of your dreams." Peggy turned and faced me with an expression that froze my eyes.

"But I guarantee you will never find a family as wonderful as ours nor a mother who cares more about you than I do."

"I will work on the paperwork and return to get you when everything is complete." Mr. Cox told me.

Mike looked down the hall, then returned and looked at Mr. Cox. "No. Just take her now. You just made things very awkward with the wife, and I promise she will not be kind if Alora stays. It is best for her to leave."

"Can I go get my things?"

"That probably isn't a good idea. I will go grab them. You stay here." Mike folded his arms above his massive belly and hardened his eyes. He never was too friendly, but now he seemed full of hate and venom.

"Can I at least tell my brothers and sisters goodbye?'

Mike scratched his armpit. "Technically, they aren't your brother and sisters, nor more than I wasn't your dad. It is best this way."

"Wow," Mr. Cox said, turning to me with what almost looked like pity.

I couldn't stop the tears that came from my eyes.

Mr. Cox's aura turned blue-gray, and he put his hand on my shoulder. He actually had a heart.

I could hear Mike's voice travel away from us. "I didn't know you had a cousin die in the foster care system."

Peggy's voice reached us. "I don't. I was lying to make a point. I can't stand that weasel of a man, Mr. Cock."

Mr. Cox lifted an eyebrow at her comment.

"Trust me, Alora, you will be better away from here."

He called me Alora!

"I am sorry I ever brought you here."

"Dr. Van Hassel said he has an airline ticket waiting for me on Sunday."

"We will have to look into that."

Mike returned, dropped a bag of crap at my feet, and turned back down the hall.

"Goodbye, Alora."

None of this had gone the way I wanted.

———◉———

AFTER A LOVELY STAY with Deborah at the crisis nursery, I landed at the Boston airport. There, in front of the luggage claim, was Dr. Van Hassel. My already elevated heart rate spiked when I saw him. I raised my left eyebrow and then turned away.

I guess I had so much delight inside me. I can't describe the feeling of freedom that bubbled in me like a freshly open can of Sprite. I had left behind the controls of the Sanibels. It felt fantastic to be liberated from the disdain of Hillary. Before my trip, I studied all about Boston and was excited to leave a small town and try my life as a city girl, although most of my time would be spent on campus.

The journey to Harvard would establish me to become someone. I refused to go by the demeaning term, Jane Doe ever again. I remembered how Peggy taught me I could be whoever I wanted. I could refine myself. I was not coming as the dumb, mute kid. I wasn't the girl locked in the basement by the Russians. I was whoever I decided to present.

So who should I be?

"Alora, you made it. I feared you wouldn't. You proved your cleverness in procuring your spot. As soon as we collect your luggage, we will drive over to Harvard. You will absolutely delight in the campus. It has a pronounced beauty to it." His aura burned emerald green. I loved the air of intelligence he carried, nothing like the folks in Box Elder County.

"I don't have any bags," I said. The crap Mike had sent with me didn't come close to fitting me. I just wore borrowed clothes at the crisis nursery and left the Sanibel junk for any kid at the nursery who might want it, which I believed would be no one.

"No clothes. That presents as a dilemma," he said. He turned to the tall man standing behind him. I hadn't realized they were together.

"Tell Erin to buy clothes for Alora straight away."

"She will be wanting the correct size, Doctor."

"What size are you, Alora?" he said, sizing me up and down with his eyes, making me feel uncomfortable and self-conscious. I really wished he would stop.

I shrugged. I was the size of ratty hand-me-downs.

"You are a brilliant mathematician. How do you not know your size?"

"I wear what is given to me." I looked down at my feet, sure that I was the biggest idiot who Dr. Van Hassel had ever met. Dr. Van Hassel dressed immaculately. No doubt he was super-rich. I felt homely and poor in his presence. He would regret flying me to the camp and send me home because I didn't fit in. Then, I would have nowhere to live. I had given up a secure home in the Sanibel house. It wasn't the most fabulous place to live, but it was safe and stable. Now, I had nothing.

What did I do?

"Erin will have to take you tonight after orientation." He looked at my attire and wrinkled his forehead. "I don't wish for you to arrive in those," he said. "First impressions go a long way."

I wanted to slink away and hide.

"Carlson, go get the car," Dr. Van Hassel told the man.

"Yes, Doctor," he said and walked away.

Dr. Van Hassel went to a newsstand and bought me an issue of *Popular Science*. Outside, Carlson stood next to a black limousine waiting for us. Adrenalin ran through me at the thought of crawling inside the expensive car. I wish all the kids at ACYI could see me now. I wished Hillary could see me.

Hillary, you are a hick. You will marry a hick. You will have hick children. You will turn out just like your mom. Not me. I am going to Harvard. I will be a renowned scientist someday. Popular Science will carry my articles.

Where did such ugliness come from? Had the Sanibel's worn off on me, or was I nasty before I lost my memory?

My skin stuck to the white leather seats inside the limo as I scooted across them. I couldn't stop smiling as I looked around. I could get used to luxury like this. Dr. Van Hassel's car trumped the shaggin' waggin' a million times over. Blue lights wrapped around the top and floorboards.

Is this real, or am I dreaming?

"I can only assume this is your first time in a limousine?" He opened the mini-fridge and pulled a flavored sparkling water out.

Pop. He undid the lid, and it sizzled as he artistically poured it into a crystal glass.

"Yes," I said as I nodded up and down. Inside the luxury mobile, he appeared even statelier than he had at my rundown Sanibel home. And yet, he still picked me.

He pulled another one out. "Would you care for a drink?" he asked.

"Yes, please!". He used prongs to drop ice into a glass.

Clink. Clink

I wouldn't have minded drinking straight out of the bottle. However, like many women in Peggy's soaps, the crystal class made me feel prestigious. I held my head high and took a tiny sip, trying not to smear my lipstick, even though I wasn't wearing lipstick. I was off on a secret rendezvous with my lover. I looked at the old professor from Harvard and shuttered. Okay, no more playing soap opera. *Gross.* Bubbles fizzled and popped in my face. I took a drink. Sweet, sugary orange fizzed in my mouth. As I swallowed, it burned its way down my throat, and a single hiccup escaped my mouth.

"Excuse me," I said as I took another sip, enjoying the bubbles again.

"You are excused." His eyebrows furrowed, and he looked out the window. I must not use hick mannerisms around him. But I didn't know how to carry myself any other way. Was Russian Alora sophisticated? Would she know how to behave around Dr. Van Hassel? I could pretend to be Russian Alora, full of class. If I acted as she would act, I could overcome the tendencies that the Sandibels had tainted me with.

After considerable silence, he said, "Now, tell me your story, Alora."

I tried to give him the shortest version. I hadn't finished when we arrived at the magnificent campus. The size, bigger than I had imagined, took my breath away.

I felt prideful showing up in a limo. I couldn't wait to have everyone see me step out of it. Maybe they would all think I was from a wealthy, well-to-do family.

-How disappointing.

Everyone showed up in limos. The difference was they stepped out in finely pressed outfits, probably straight off the designer rack. I wore peach stretchy pants with a small hole in the knee. My oversized T-shirt had a stupid cat on it. I didn't even like cats.

Carlson parked next to the curb in front of a dorm. The red brick building rose several stories high. Each window had white trim around it.

"Do you want to go inside or take a small walk to stretch from the long flight?"

A gaggle of girls stood outside the dorm. Even though we were still in the limo, I could smell their perfume, feel their glares, and bask in their disdain. Regardless, I know I made it up, but wasn't ready for it.

As we walked, I could feel the power and energy of education permeating the grounds. The phenomenon was truth and not something I made up. A low-frequency vibration came from the acquisition and construction of knowledge.

Am I really going to spend the rest of my summer here? I stopped breathing. -among order and not chaos. Something tickled my arm, and I swatted at it, used to Mantua mosquitos. My fingers flicked an Eastern Tailed Blue butterfly, and its wings crinkled inwards, and it fell to the grass.

Oh, no! I would never kill a butterfly on purpose. I bent down to look at it.

"Alora," Dr. Van Hassel said, obviously annoyed by me stopping. I needed just a few seconds to fix the butterfly's wings and bring it back to life.

"Alora, do try to keep up and resist the urge to stop and observe every blade of grass."

First, I had to take care of Dr. Van Hassel. I peered into him and applied my theory of time, which I had created over the summer at the library. I attempted to slow Dr. Van Hassel's reality of time, but I was unsure if it would work. Dr. Van Hassel became stiff, almost statue-like, with extremely slow movements. I quickly scooped the butterfly up and healed it in my hand. It tickled me with its fluttering wings against my skin. I watched it, and then it flew away. I joined Dr. Van Hassel's side and restored his perception of time. He seemed oblivious to what had just happened.

As we walked, my attention turned to the old and distinguished buildings, reminding me of a picture I had seen of the English Parliament building. Again, a flash of joy rippled through me. And to think, Peggy wanted to withhold this from me. I had to push Peggy from my mind, for thinking of her made me want to cry.

After all, she was the only mother I knew.

Eventually, we returned to the dorm. "This is where you will stay for the next month," Dr. Van Hassel said as he escorted me in.

"I want you to know, Jane." I shot him a look when he used my generic name. "I mean, Alora. I want you to know I *never* pick up students for these things. I usually have my secretary run errands like this."

"Then why did you get me?" I nimbly asked. A girl behind him raised an eyebrow at me, and I knew she didn't want me there. Who would? I looked like a hick, not a wealthy scholar.

"Because you are highly important." How could such a powerful man think that about me? No one else in the world did. "I have had the opportunity to meet some very bright, intellectual students. I have reviewed test scores and monitored program placement. I have never seen anyone with the potential you possess. I realized from your story there is more to you than anyone knows. I want to be with you every step of the way as you unlock your pathway to greatness."

His praise made me feel warm all over despite my dumb outfit.

———◆———

DR. VAN HASSEL INTRODUCED me to my new roommate.

She swung her left hip out and placed her hand on it. "Nope. My parents paid for a private dorm room." Her orange aura reminded me of Mr. Cox's.

"Sharon Winchester. I am I am Dr. Van Hassel." Her color drained to a dingy white, the color of Mike's dirty tank tops. "I will kick you out of the program if you do not contain your emotions."

That was all it took. Sharon returned to organizing her drawers, trying not to look at us. I couldn't wait to spend the rest of the summer with another fan of my hate club.

"Can I assume I won't hear another word about this from you?" Dr. Van Hassel said to her in a low voice.

She looked up, "Yes sir, sorry sir."

Dr. Van Hassel left, and I had nothing to do but watch Sharon. I didn't have clothes or things to organize. Her dull, long black hair flopped over her face as she moved around the room. The room felt too tight for us. The Sanibel's shed was larger than our dorm room. She gave me the evil eye after Dr. Van Hassel left, with bulging eyes that seemed to pop out of her head. I hated it! She was going to make my time at the dorm very uncomfortable.

"How do you know Dr. Van Hassel? Are you his niece or something?"

"No."

"Then how do you know him?"

"I don't know. I met him a couple of days ago when he came to my house and invited me to this camp." I looked down. I couldn't handle her eyes.

"You are lying," Sharon said.

"Why would you think I am lying? Did you not see him escort me here?" Sharon talked down to me, reminding me of Principal Schimdt and Hillary. Why did I get stuck rooming with her out of all the kids in the camp?

"Yeah, but that isn't how Dr. Van Hassel works. He doesn't recruit people for this camp. Anyone who goes here has to apply for it and then take a rigorous test. It's a lengthy application process, and only some people make it. Only the best of the best."

"Do you consider yourself the best of the best?" I asked. I couldn't believe I was being so bold. My skin tingled, and I looked away.

"You better know it," she said hotly, raising her head high. "I am a Winchester," she continued. "I come from a line of the best family in Boston. My pedigree can be traced to having Harvard graduates as far back as the mid seventeen hundreds. There hasn't been a generation who has skipped coming here."

"Wow," I said. "That is quite a heritage you have." I was so intrigued by her family line I forgot we were not friends, but she quickly reminded me of our animosity.

"Indeed," she replied, lifting her chin even higher in the air. "And where do you hail from?"

I didn't know what to tell her. Should I have claimed Mantua as my home? Maybe Bountiful, since I was found there. I felt more connected to Mantua. I wondered if I should claim Russia, for I was sure my roots traced me back there.

"Russia," I finally decided upon. It sounded more exotic than Utah.

"Are you a communist?"

"No, that is where my roots trace back. I come from Mantua, Utah."

"Never heard of it," she said as she kept her nose up. She must have thought it wasn't an important place if she didn't know about it.

"Utah, what do I know about that state?" she thought out loud for a moment. "Ah yes, the union of the Central Pacific and Union Pacific Railroads on May tenth, eighteen sixty-nine. The Great Salt Lake is in Utah, and it is roughly twenty-one hundred square miles. Utah has five national parks: Zion, Bryce Canyon, Capitol Reef, Arches, and Canyonlands. Utah was acquired by the United States in eighteen forty eighty in a treaty ending a war. Do you know what war that was?"

"No," I said. She certainly knew more about Utah than I did.

"It was the Mexico War," she said smartly. She continued as if she was impressing me. "Utah comes from the Ute Indian tribe. It is the eleventh-largest state in the United States. I bet you didn't even know about your own state."

I might not have known trivial facts like she did, but I had the world map downloaded into my brain. I bet she didn't.

The landline in our dorm rang. Sharon answered it. "Yes, no, this is not her. Hold on..." She handed the phone to me. Her bulging eyes swam in hate.

After I hung the phone up, I said, "That was Erin, Dr. Van Hassel's secretary. She wanted me to tell you to lead us to the Epigaea Repens room. Oh yeah, and she is taking me shopping at 6." I could dish out snoot.

***

I PRACTICALLY HAD TO run to keep up with Sharon. She tried to ditch me, but I wouldn't let her. I bet she had spent her summer memorizing the campus maps because it felt like we were going through a labyrinth to get to the Epigaea Repens room. When we got there, we mingled with around a hundred other students. I was momentarily confused because I was sure Dr. Van Hassel had said they only let twenty students in a year, but then I remembered there were older years as well. We were all meeting together for an orientation meeting and luncheon. I had lost Sharon in the crowd, which I was glad for because I didn't want to sit by her, and I was sure she felt the same.

The room smelt like overcooked broccoli and scorched chicken. It wouldn't taste as good as Peggy's cooking, but at least I would get a larger portion. Perhaps while I was there, I would gain a little weight and not look like a starving orphan.

I stood in the small line of the first years to pick up my summer agenda. When it became my turn, I said.

"Funk, Alora." The guy flipped through the agendas, not finding mine.

"This is the first-year line," he said as if I was an idiot.

"Oh, my mistake. I think it might be under Jane Doe," I replied.

"Jane Doe. Are you Alora or Jane?"

"Both," I said. "It is complicated."

He searched again. "Nope, neither name. Maybe it got sorted in the wrong year. Go try another year."

I ended up standing in each line. I felt stupid in the older lines because I was obviously too young for them. I had several kids try to direct me back to the first year. After wasting time in every line, I finally went empty-handed and sat beside a stranger. Fifteen minutes later, the MC started.

"You guys worked hard to get here. When I say you belong here, I mean it. This is not a place for simple minds. It is a breeding institute for the leading intellects in the nation. You will go on to become surgeons, rocket scientists, and the greatest minds of our country in many fields. It will all begin with the roots you sow over the next few weeks and your continuing years in this summer science camp."

His speech bored me, and I nodded off a couple of times. I must have been experiencing jet lag. A new speaker came and explained how the cafeteria program worked. We were given the rules, including absolutely no leaving of the campus. We were also warned we were not allowed to enter the opposite genders' dorms. It was immediate dismissal from the program with no refunds if we were found in such.

"I know that was much information to take in," he said. "Without further ado, let me introduce the man behind the dream. This program would not exist if Dr. Van Hassel hadn't founded it." The room became silent. Everyone stopped eating, staring with mouths wide open, reminding me of Sanibels. Dr. Van Hassel stepped to the pulpit. He had complete respect, admiration, and attention from the room.

His was a drawn-out speech. I felt like I was the only one there who was tired and bored. Everyone sat erect as they clung to each word out of his mouth. After he rambled for quite some time, he said.

"Open your agendas. We will expect strict adherence to this agenda. This is your life. You will do nothing without first checking your agenda." The statement stirred a ripple of chatter and the sound of rustling paper.

"Quiet!" he demanded. Everything went still. "There can't possibly be anything more important than my words at this moment." The guy up at the pulpit didn't seem like the same caring man who came to my Mantua home. The Dr. Van Hassel at the podium kind of scared me.

"When it says homework time, you will do homework and nothing else. You won't be writing letters to your mommy and daddy. You will be doing homework. You won't be flirting and being silly. You will be doing homework. Do I make myself clear?" he shouted into the microphone. It was so loud that many people cupped their ears. How did that man have patience for ME?

"I almost forgot," he said as he reached under the podium. His voice softened with his following words. "Alora, I have your agenda. I meant to give it to you in the limousine. Come up and get it."

Everyone wildly searched the auditorium, looking for what peon was on a first-name basis with our king. I slowly stood up, the chair loudly scraping the floor and ringing a metallic grind. With all eyes on me, the walk seemed painfully long. My stupid shoes squeaked with every step I took. My legs stiffened up on me, not wanting to move. I couldn't believe I had to go up in my horrific outfit. I couldn't wait for the promised new clothes. The walk took two eternities; my head became light, and my vision closed to only a slit of light. I couldn't let myself pass out. I reached Dr. Van Hassel, who handed me my agenda and patted my back. It shook my hand. Puke rose up my throat.

No! Not Now! I couldn't puke in front of all these elitists. I needed to redefine Alora, not come as the same loser from Mantua. I turned my back to the crowd and swallowed the horrific, hot, thick sludge. A little dribbled down my chin, and I wiped it on the back of my agenda.

"If you want to make it through this camp and be invited to return next year," Dr. Van Hassel bellowed. I turned back and refused to look at anyone as I walked toward my seat. Did they know what I had just done? "Then I suggest you all keep a close eye on Alora Funk. You will want her in your group. You will want her on your team. If you want to succeed, you will fight for her acknowledgment."

My head pounded, and I sat but only managed to get half my butt on the chair, and I slid to the floor. Thankfully, Dr. Van Hassel didn't see, but I am sure everyone else did. Gray dust bunnies clung to my peach pants as I pulled myself up and properly sat in my chair. Heat burned all over me, and I am sure if you had put an egg on my skin, I would have fried it.

I buried my head in my hands. Why did Dr. Van Hassel speak such mighty words about me? Wasn't I the same lowly girl who had been accused of cheating not very long ago? How fast my world changed.

After our luncheon, they separated us into years. The first-year students were given a tour of the campus.

I think the campus is more enormous than Mantua. Could it be? I would have to research that. *How will I ever remember my way around?* As we snaked our way through it, a thought hit me. I was trying to grasp things with my logical mind, not my intellectual mind. I was distinguishing between the two abilities. My logical mind was what I used for everyday things. I am sure it was what everyone used. But, when I solved math equations or looked at maps, I could feel myself switch to my intellectual mind. What I needed to learn was how to stay more permanently in my intellectual mind.

Once I switched to my intellectual mind, I mapped the campus, recording everything I saw. My mind created several maps, and I am not sure how I did it, but I had aerial views, ground views, and topography views. They were rather brilliant. Maybe I already had the Harvard Campus map downloaded to my brain.

I was excited to find a way to use my new enlightenment better. If I could learn to manage my abilities, I was sure I could make myself powerful. The idea felt astounding because not long ago, I was the stupid, dumb mute with the intelligence of a fourth grader, a nobody. I would show them!

As we went around, I noticed eyes on me at all times. Since I had personally known Dr. Van Hassel, it made me an instant celebrity. No one talked to me, but they must have waited for the right moment.

After the long tour, I returned to my dorm to find Sharon on her bed. She actually looked pleasant, not wearing her scowl from before.

"Did you have a good lunch?" she asked.

"Yup," I coolly responded. I wasn't sure if I was ready to be friends yet.

"Were you able to figure out the campus?" She really sounded sincere. She opened a crinkly wrapper and pulled out a candy bar, stuffing almost the whole thing in her mouth at once. My tongue salivated as I watched her, wanting one myself. *If she offered, I would take a bite.*

"I am sure I will manage fine," I said, softening my tone. Maybe she had another candy bar for me.

"Oh, good. I memorized the campus before I got here." I could hardly understand her with her mouth so full. I bet most Winchesters didn't talk with their mouths full. She acted more like a Sanibel. "My brother Ronald said it was so hard to memorize. He kept getting lost. I am above getting lost, so I took the time to study it. Did you study it?" she asked.

"I really didn't have the time. I found out I was coming on Friday. But it's okay because I already have the campus figured out."

"I still don't get how you found out Friday. Everyone applies a year in advance. Were you put on the alternate schedule?"

"No, I never applied. To tell you the truth, I hadn't even heard about the camp until Dr. Van Hassel came to my home Friday, begging me to come." I said, begging with an air of pride.

"That is an injustice!" Sharon screamed. I jumped at her sudden outburst. "Everyone has to apply." She suddenly softened her tone, probably not wanting to upset me. Since Dr. Van Hassel had told everyone to be friends with me, I think she planned on securing the title of my *best friend.* She could start by giving me a candy bar. "I am not mad at you, just at the system."

"Fair," I responded.

We turned to the knock at the door. I opened it while Sharon stayed on her bed. A middle-aged woman with salt and pepper hair stood on the other side.

"Hello, Alora," she said to me. "I am Erin, Dr. Van Hassel's personal secretary. He has asked me to take you shopping."

I turned to Sharon. She sat on her bed with a look of utter envy on her face. Her big eyes looked pitiful. I flashed a smile and left with Erin.

———◆———

I SIGHED AND TOOK A pack of cinnamon mints from my pant pocket. I wanted gum, but Erin had said it was banned from campus. I doubted that. I could hardly keep my eyes open as I walked into the dorm. At least there wouldn't be a million Sanibels keeping me awake. The shopping had milked out the last of my energy. Back at the dorm, I fell asleep the moment my head hit the pillow. The following day, I had the enormous task of figuring out what to wear from my new clothes. I finally decided on a cream-colored blouse with brown pants. I felt dignified. I couldn't believe I had new clothes. Erin hadn't exactly picked out stylish clothes that the kids in Mantua would wear, but I didn't care. They were new!

Sharon seemed torn between her feelings for me. I could tell she hated me because I had been forced into her dorm room. On the other hand, she knew Dr. Van Hassel highly valued me, and therefore, I might play out to be used as a pawn to her advancement at Harvard. She had told me every kid tried to get noticed by Dr. Van Hassel because he could be the key to instant acceptance to the graduate program.

"Let's go to breakfast together," she offered.

Where would she fit in the social hierarchy at ACYI? She would definitely be a nerd, but here at Harvard, she seemed to think she was top material.

"Okay," I said.

"We'll hurry," she barked as if she struggled to be kind to me. I was completely ready, but she still hadn't put her shoes and socks on. It wasn't me whom we waited for.

In the cafeteria, they had the tables sectioned by years. Ten kids already sat at our first year's table. We joined them. Several kids told me to sit by them. I glanced at Sharon, who rolled those bulgy eyes, most likely peeved that I got all the attention. She had to be a nerd where she had come from and should be used to it. I found a spot where Sharon could sit by me, but she sat as far away from me as possible.

After breakfast, we started our academic day. Monday-Friday was the same for the four weeks.

*0800*****Breakfast*

*0830*****History of Science (Science Building 3: room 302) Dr. Laudel*

*0930*****Break*

*0915*****Communities of Knowledge, Science, Religion, and Culture. (Science Building 2: room 222) Dr. Morris.*

*1015*****Break*

*1030*****Study Group*

*1130*****Biomedical Science, with emphasis on Anatomy, Microbiology, and Pathophysiology. (Biomedical Building 3: lab 8) Dr. Powers*

*1230*****Lunch Break*

*1300***** Biomedical Science, with emphasis on Anatomy, Microbiology, and Pathophysiology. (Biomedical Building 3: lab 8) Dr. Powers*

*1445*****Break*

*1500*****Scientific Writing. (English Building 1: room 101) Dr. Murphy*

*1600*****Break*

*1615*****Chemistry (Math Building 1: Chemistry lab2) Dr. Moody*

*1745*****Dinner Break*

*1815*****Science Engineering (Science Building 3: engineering lab 5) Dr. Scholfield*
*1915*****Break*
*1930*****Math (Math Building 1) Dr. Horrison*
*2030*****Homework*
*2130****Bed*

———◉———

THE SCHEDULE MADE ME tired looking at it. When I was invited to summer camp, I imagined it like the campground at Mantua or the *Parent Trap* movie. I had been bored at the Sanibels, but suddenly, I wanted that lifestyle again. I wanted to fish or explore the mountains. The schedule was too much, and I was angry at myself for fighting to be at Harvard. The agenda seemed like a nightmare. It made school feel like playtime. The other kids had chosen to be here, but they knew what they were getting into.

I want to go home.

Saturday and Sunday weren't as grueling, but there wasn't much of a rest

*0800*****Breakfast*
*0845*****Study Group Rotation 1*
*1000*****Break*
*1030*****Study Group Rotation 2*
*1130*****Physical Fitness*
*1230*****Lunch Break*
*1300*****Study Group Rotation 3*
*1400*****Break*
*1415*****Study Group Rotation 4*
*1515*****Break*
*1530*****Guest Speaker (Science Lecture Hall)*
*1745*****Dinner Break*
*1800*****Personal Mediation/Reflection Time*

*1900*****Homework*
*2030*****Break*
*2045*****Homework*
*2245*****Bed*

The classes were long, and I often watched the other students. Some of them scribbled down every word the professor said. Others watched intently but never wrote a thing down. A few doodled in their notebook. Their attention looked like it was somewhere else. Then there was Teddy.

Teddy stood taller than the rest of us, and I could measure him in my head. He was six feet exactly, even though he claimed six-foot-one inch. He had long, shaggy hair, and he always wore black. Most of the kids in the program dressed sharply. The girls wore blouses, skirts, or nice pants. Many boys wore ties and white shirts, polos, and jackets. Everyone looked slick except Teddy. He didn't seem to want to be there. Had his parents forced him to come? He probably missed his girlfriend. Teddy tried to sleep in as many classes as he could. Most of the professors didn't care, but Dr. Powers never allowed it, and he would scold Teddy every time he caught him drifting to sleep.

I had free time in each class because I quickly discovered that I didn't have to pay attention. I became quicker at pulling up charts, diagrams, and definitions of everything taught to us. I loved how cells became 3D in my mind, exposing deep into their lipid layers and ribosomes, lysosomes, and everything making up a cell. It was astounding. I could unravel DNA, break apart its hydrogen bonds, and explore its nitrogen nucleotides.

Who had I been?

The lectures bored me, for I probably knew more than they did on subjects. I daydreamed a lot, watched people, and even joined the doodling crowd. The professors *loved* calling upon me for answers to their questions. I don't know if they were trying to stump me, trying to show me off, or what, but I was asked three times the number of questions as the rest of the class was.

"Alora, Which planet of our solar system moves around the sun at a speed of 36,840 km/h?"

"What?" I asked, getting caught again in another daydream.

"You think you know everything," some would say. What a difference from being the stupid girl. I think I swung to the opposite end of the spectrum of the social line, stupid to brilliant, yet I wasn't liked on either end.

Was I?

My very favorite of the classes ended up being chemistry with an emphasis of microbiology. When Dr. Moody talked about the simple properties of matter and chemical bonds, I could see the molecular makeup of matter. I could actually see the atoms and molecules with their electrons and bonds. I could see photochemical reactions and oxidation-reduction reactions; I could see everything! I found I had an extensive knowledge base in my mind. After I left chemistry, I would forever be looking at things through a molecular eye.

I was dying to talk to him during Dr. Moody's second lecture.

"Dr. Moody, can I ask you a few questions?" I said after everyone left his classroom.

"Oh, little lady, you don't want to be late for dinner." He addressed me in that same cartoon voice Peggy liked to use. He must have been forced to teach this summer camp, which showed. He didn't even glance up to look at me. His musk burnt my eyes. Did this man, I mean professor, ever shower?

"That's okay. Just a few questions, please?" I stammered with a soft, weak voice.

"Go ahead," he said, looking at me for the first time. He had a golden-yellow aura. He was probably in his late fifties, with a round face and glasses at the tip of his nose. His hair was black, with a little gray.

"I have a pretty good understanding of chemistry," I said

"Do you?"

-What a jerk. I didn't like how he said it, but I kept going. "It seems like so many things have the same molecular structure. Take hydrochloric acid, for instance. If you add one oxygen molecule, it becomes hypochlorous acid. If you add two, it becomes chlorous acid. If you add three, it becomes chloric acid, and if you add four..."

"It becomes perchloric acid," Dr. Moody said, finishing my thought. "Pretty amazing, isn't it?"

"Yes, it is astounding. Could we completely change matter if we could move atoms around in similar structures?"

I thought about how I had turned garbage into food. *Why haven't I experimented more with this?*

"Yes, we can and do it all the time, but it's more than changing or adding atoms. You must account for bonds and making and breaking new bonds."

"But, if you knew the fingerprint to every molecule, then do you think one could change, let's say, a rock to bread."

"There is recorded history of a man in Jerusalem who did it two thousand years ago," Dr. Moody said. His eyes softened, and his voice regulated. He now spoke to me more as a student and not an idiot.

"Wow, what other things did this man do?"

"Some say he helped create this world by using all the laws of chemistry."

"I am not following you," I said.

"His name was Jesus Christ. Have you heard of him?"

"Sure, I have," I responded, feeling a little stupid for not knowing that.

"Mercy, me. We have failed you," I could hear Peggy chastising me in my head for not recognizing Dr. Moody was referencing God.

"Do you really think Jesus created this earth?"

"In conflict to many of my co-colleagues, I do."

"I thought science was about the big bang theory, about the earth creating itself," I said.

"Do you believe that?" Dr. Moody responded.

"Well, no. I have a good model of the Big Bang theory in my head, but it doesn't equal out to what they say it does.

"Precisely my thoughts indeed. This world is made up of solid scientific and mathematical laws. You can't cheat the laws. You can't bend them. They are set in stone. I can't believe -poof, a bang created laws that formed our whole earth, solar system, and the universe. There is no way. Take the human body, for instance. Everything in it works together and depends on all the other organs and molecule structures from within. If one system fails, the others start failing. The body has great safeguards where it can adjust and fix itself. That isn't evolution. It didn't spawn from a one-cell ameba. That is Science, and Science has laws," he said. I noticed as he explained his thoughts his aura was white. Many of the professor's auras turned white when they taught or lectured.

"So, you are telling me you don't believe in evolution?" I asked. I was astounded to speak to someone with a doctorate in chemistry who didn't believe in evolution. We had learned in school how evolution was religion to scientists.

"I do believe in evolution, for we have strong evidence it exists. Take the Tupinambis teguixin, for instance. Are you familiar with them?"

"Yes, the whiptail lizard. They are all females, but when a male isn't around, one female will become the male," I had finished his sentence with knowledge I didn't even know I had. I loved how I was evolving.

"Precisely, you are well educated. I suppose that is why you are here. I believe in evolution, for our species depend upon it, but I believe in structure and no happenstance. This world didn't create itself with all its laws from a big bang. A mighty scientist orchestrated it. God is that scientist who believes and celebrates Science like the best of us. I don't see how the two can't coincide, but believe you me, I have had my share of arguments on this subject." Dr. Moody shifted his weight in his seat. Meanwhile, my legs burned, and I wanted to sit down but ignored them.

"So, you believe God created this world by manipulating matter?" I asked.

"Precisely."

"Do you believe I could manipulate matter and do the same?" I asked.

"Well, it would take great effort and study, but many have done it. Being at this summer camp is a good step in that direction."

Dr. Moody looked at his watch. "Listen, little lady, I hate to make you miss dinner. They have you on a tight schedule. You better run along so you don't miss it."

"Oh, but I am not done talking about this." I had so much I wanted to ask him.

"If you were a regular student, I would schedule a time for us to meet, but your agenda doesn't make time for such matters."

"Can I meet with you during dinner tomorrow? Maybe I can take an extra sandwich at lunch and eat it tomorrow during our appointment."

"Well, if you are so anxious, let's make it happen."

———— ◈ ————

BY THE TIME I REACHED the cafeteria, I had missed dinner. My stomach growled and rebelled in loud gurgles as I went to science engineering hungry.

I could hardly concentrate the rest of the day because my mind was about molecules. I made an inventory of all the elements in the room. It was like a giant pantry, with endless molecules available. I really wanted to rearrange the matter in my mind and see if I could change things around. I had done it before without knowing how. As my mind awakened, I wanted to understand how to do it better. I couldn't wait to visit with Dr. Moody again.

On the third day, it felt like dinner time would never get there. I was so antsy for my appointment with Dr. Moody. It finally came, and he took me into his office, where he had set up a little table. A towel was laid out with his pasta on top with an empty plate for me. I took my warm turkey sandwich out of the backpack. I had grabbed it at lunch and stuffed it in there. The lettuce was wilted, and the bread soggy.

"I admire your interest in chemistry," Dr. Moody said through a mouth full of pasta. Little pieces of his meal broke off as he spoke and torpedoed my way. It was gross. One landed on my arm, leaving a wet spot behind. Another landed on my sandwich. If I weren't so starving, I would have thrown the sandwich away, but I had already missed dinner the night before, and I wasn't about to do it again.

"I suppose I should know the name of the person I am dining with tonight," he said, shoveling in another mouthful of pasta. He didn't even notice a piece fell onto his lap. "But don't expect me to remember it."

"I am Alora Funk."

He dropped his fork and stared at me for a moment. "So, you are her. I guess I will remember your name. Dr. Van Hassel has some high hopes for you. I have never seen him take a personal interest in one of his students before."

"Why do you think that is?" I asked.

"Because he knows you have a sharp mind. We were all told to do whatever it took to help you meet your full potential."

I blushed.

"What can I help you with, Ms. Funk?" I saw something change across his face.

"Well, I feel like it would be easy to manipulate matter, real easy-actually, but I want to understand more about it."

"You think it's easy, but you... You've lost me."

"Well, I can see the atoms in everything around us, which are plentiful. I don't know how to grasp those atoms and secure them to change them."

"What do you mean?"

"Well, I am discovering I have two types of minds in my head. I know it sounds weird. I don't really have two brains, but it's more like I have two brain functions. One of them, I call my intellectual mind. Looking at things through it, I can see the molecules that make up the structure. I don't know if I am seeing the molecular structure of an object or if my mind is showing me what the molecular structure should be."

"Energy," Dr. Moody said. He now talked to me more like a colleague instead of a student. I scanned the room, embarrassed to look at him.

"Energy for what?" I looked at him, and his eyes locked onto mine. His white aura mixed into my blue aura, and soon mine was white like his.

"For your question. You said you didn't know how to grasp the atoms and secure them to change them. It takes energy to change and create bonds."

"Energy," I repeated. "I really did know that. I hadn't thought of it. How simple. Now, I feel foolish."

Since the hospital, I had seen object's energy fields. We all are made up of energy and the ability to regenerate it. If I could manipulate the energy fields, then I would be able to accomplish wielding matter.

Back at the Sanibel's, I had changed garbage into a feast. I had done it at the time without knowing the process. I must have known how to do it before my memory swipe. Somehow, I had just made it happen. Now, I wanted to know every part of the process.

Dinner ended way too soon, and I found myself back in class. Instead of focusing on lectures, I studied the energy fields around everything. Somehow, I had to find a way to manipulate my energy to reach over and move matter around. I kept trying, feeling I was so close to success.

The next day, I again met Dr. Moody in his office for dinner. I pulled out a tuna sandwich.

"Is that from lunch?" he asked me as he took a bite of his steak.

"Yeah," I said, taking a bite of my warm sandwich.

"STOP! YOU CAN'T EAT THAT!" he shouted. I startled by his yell. "You will get sick. It has mayonnaise in it. Mayonnaise spoils if you leave it out of the fridge. It is a great medium for incubating bacteria." I thought about the turkey sandwich I had eaten the night before. I hadn't gotten sick, and it had mayonnaise on it.

He pushed his steak over to me. "Here, eat this instead."

"No, I can't eat your dinner."

"I can grab a burger after this, but you can't. You'll go hungry, and I am not letting you eat your sandwich with spoiled mayonnaise on it."

I took his steak. I had been drooling for it since I walked in. I thought about protesting more, but the steak was too tempting, and I accepted it. I sunk my teeth into the thick, juicy meat. A savory sensation exploded in my mouth!

"Is there anything I can do to help?" he asked.

"Do you have a book with all the chemical structures of molecules?" I said with a mouth full of food. I tried to swallow it quickly.

"Sure. I have several. Let me go get them for you." He went and rummaged through his shelves and pulled out four very large textbooks. He plopped them down in front of me: the top one read, *Molecular Phenomena of Unbelievable Complexity- a Study in Structure.* The books were too big for me to lug around, so Dr. Moody promised to drop them off in my dorm.

Chapter 8

A SNAIL COULD CRAWL faster than the first week went. I had a love/hate relationship for the camp. I hated how every minute was dictated for us. Everything we did had to be on their agenda, or it didn't happen, except for my nightly dinners with Dr. Moody during the week. I had already found a way to loop the system.

I was surprised at how much the other kids complained. I understood their complaints, because I felt the same stresses as well, but the rest of them shouldn't have complained in my opinion. They had worked hard to be there. To them, it was the pinnacle career move of their teen years. Their parents had spent good money to have them there. For some, fifteen-thousand-dollars was change, and meant nothing, but I had learned a few of their moms had gotten jobs just so that they could send their kids to this camp.

I later learned from Dr. Moody how my scholarship was granted by Dr. Van Hassel himself. I wasn't sure why he took such a great interest in me.

During my homework and meditation time, I flipped through the chemistry books.

"You aren't even taking time to read them," Sharon commented as she watched me.

"I don't need to read them. I am making mental notes, kind of like taking a mental picture."

She bent over and looked at the chemical structures on the page. I could smell the apple shampoo in her hair. At times, I snuck some when I showered.

"There is no way you are memorizing one thing out of that book," she said with disdain.

"This is already my second book, and I memorized everything in the first one."

"You're full of it."

"If you don't believe it, pick it up and ask me anything. Go ahead, anything. It is over there on my pillow."

"No, I don't want to," she said.

"Then stop bothering me."

"Well, I can't concentrate on studying with you flipping those pages like that. You must stop."

"I am not stopping until I have them all memorized," I kept my eyes on the book as we fought.

"Why are you wasting your time on that? Don't you realize on Monday we have tests in all of our classes? If you don't get an eighty-five percent or better, then they will kick you out of camp." She fluffed her pillow, then said, "Which I hope they do."

I didn't care if I got kicked out. I decided I was ready to go home and finish enjoying my summer. I would never complain about being bored at the Sanibels again. I missed all the free time I had there. I missed going out on the reservoir. I missed Athena. In my opinion, Harvard Summer Camp was way too rigid for children. But I knew I wouldn't get kicked out, for I planned on getting a hundred percent on everything. That would show Sharon.

The tests came, and they were easy and quick for me. I finished the tests early and then would sit there and study matter. I watched some of the kids cry. I could remember what it felt like not understanding the subject, so I tried not to act pompous or anything.

———— ◉ ————

"I FINISHED THE BOOKS, and you are free to pick them up whenever you want," I told Dr. Moody over almond-crusted halibut. He started bringing me dinners along with his.

"I take it the reading was a bit above your level," he said with a mouthful of food. I hated it when he talked while eating; he always spit food my way.

"Au contraire," I said. "It all made sense, and I have it all stored in my mind." I tapped my forehead and left a smear of grease from the halibut. I took my linen napkin and wiped my head. Did Dr. Moody use linen napkins at home?

"There is no way. How do you do it?"

"I take a mental picture of everything."

"Mental picture?"

"Yes, much like a camera."

"And how do you recall it when you need it?"

"I think of it, and then it is there. I work much faster than a computer."

"Is that what you have done with everything they teach you here? I hear from the other professors it appears as if you know everything."

"Yes. It doesn't take me long to recall things. I believe most of my information was stored there some time ago because I seem to know almost everything they are teaching."

"Have you always been like this?"

"No, a couple of months ago, I was on a fourth-grade level on everything. But suddenly, I have entered enlightenment, which seems to be no bounds to my understanding and knowledge base."

"You are telling me you went from being behind in everything to knowing it all in a matter of months?"

"Well, yes and no. About six months ago, they found me in a cement room hooked up to drugs, which kept me in a chemically induced coma. I was being watched by a Russian couple. When I left there, I had no knowledge of my life to that point. It was all erased. But, suddenly, my intellectual side is waking up, and I am finding a wealth of knowledge in it. I suspect I must have been learning all these things before I had been chemically induced."

"Wow, I see, I see," he said as he rubbed his chin. "Yours is quite a story."

——————⬤——————

WHEN I RETURNED TO my dorm that night, the books were gone.

By Friday, I was deathly bored. I wanted to return to Mantua, for I missed my free time and being outside. I didn't feel like I was learning anything. Every now and then, a new concept would be introduced, and I would log it away with the rest, but it was so rare it wasn't worth all the time I was devoted to the camp for a sliver of new knowledge.

Having access to so much information in my brain made me wonder about my life even more. How did I seem to have a mental reference to everything science and math-related? A couple of months ago, I didn't even know what simple things were, and now I could solve math equations faster than a computer, and not simple equations either, very complex ones. I had charts and systems stored in my head. Where had it all come from? If I could access all of that, why couldn't I retrieve my memories?

With all my capacity for retaining knowledge so quickly, the kids in the study groups focused on me. They knew I had the definition for anything. During groups, they picked my brain; however, they had learned if they needed to understand a concept, not to ask me, for I had a difficult time explaining it. I was good for facts and equations. I was not good at teaching.

It was Friday, the last class for the day: math. We worked on a combination of advanced calculus with a bit of geometry mixed in. I fought sleep and homesickness. Who would have thought I would have missed the Sanibels so fiercely? Droning the teacher out, I tried to find access to my energy. I could feel it, sensing its vibrations and strength. I needed to control it, spending all week trying to link into it, when suddenly -there in math- I tapped the access line to my energy! I could feel it. I could sense it. I could shape it. In a way, it felt like another appendage of mine, sort of like hands. I named my energy appendage my Zen.

With my Zen, I grasped the energy field around my pencil and lifted it. There it was, floating in front of me! It was the most remarkable moment of my life! My arm hairs stood up; a rush of pure joy burst through me. I was holding the pencil by its energy -but to the naked eye- it looked like it was levitating. A sense of magic overwhelmed me; although it wasn't magic, it was simple science, so simple and yet so complicated and out of reach to most humans. My discovery thrilled me; excited me, realizing this was only the beginning. I could control things! I wanted to jump out of my chair and scream in joy, but I couldn't because I didn't want to draw attention to what I was capable of.

Searching for another object to experiment with, I looked at the teacher. Devious feelings entered as I thought about experimenting on him. The idea was so funny I lacked the will to stop myself. Releasing my Zen, I grabbed the energy field around Dr. Harrison. My heart pounded when I realized I was dominating his energy. Instead of levitating him, like I wanted to, I carried some of his energy back with me. With his energy field markedly depleted, Dr. Harrison collapsed to the ground. At the same time, his energy exploded within me and shot me out of my chair. No one noticed me because all eyes were on Dr. Harrison on the ground. My nerve endings rang with all the added energy, and my muscles spasmed. I didn't know how to tame such an influx. My mind felt open, clarity, full of strength. It was the greatest high I had ever felt. My heart pounded wildly, trying to compensate for the onslaught of energy and work.

Meanwhile, several kids had run to Dr. Harrison's side, fearing he was having a heart attack. Scared at what I had done, I quickly sent his energy back. His body jerked twice on the floor as the energy returned to him, sending him flying several feet to his left. He went from pale and frail-looking to vibrant and pink.

"I am sorry, class. I don't know what happened to me," he said, pulling himself off the ground. Even Teddy woke up. All eyes were on Dr. Harrison. "Are you okay?" a student asked. "Should I go and get the nurse?"

"I feel fine. Thanks for asking. I had momentarily lost all of my energy. I don't need the nurse. I just started a workout program, and I might have overdone it on my morning run."

It took him a few minutes to regain his composure. When he had, he went back to teaching. I shook because of what I had done. It had worked! I had controlled his energy. My mind whirled with thought. If I could command the energy of anything around me, my possibilities were endless as to what I could do with that type of power. I hungered to know if I could do it again.

I couldn't sit contently with my discovery. I snaked my Zen out and grabbed Dr. Harrison's energy again, bringing it back to me. He fell to the ground, depleted. Simultaneously, I was thrown out of my seat by the addition of his energy, bumping my head on the leg of the empty chair next to me. My head pounded. No one seemed to notice me in the back since all eyes were on our teacher. Every cell within me vibrated at the increase. I wanted to run fifty laps around the room. I sat up and looked at Dr. Harrison. He looked dead. Had I taken too much? I quickly returned it.

When I returned Dr. Harrison's energy, he looked sheepish to be on the floor again. Sharon ran to his side, helping him stand up. "Are you sure you don't need to see the nurse?" she asked. It was the first time I had ever seen concern in her bulging eyes.

He looked embarrassed. "No, I am fine now. Fine. If it happens again, then maybe I will."

As much as I wanted to do it again, I didn't. As he returned to his lecture, I ran experiments in my head.

SATURDAY, I WAS IN my first study group rotation. The program leaders thought we would benefit from studying together in small groups of five and then rotating and changing the groups around. They wanted us to have the chance to tap into everyone's different viewpoints and thoughts. I hated study groups because no one left me alone. Instead of studying things out, they asked me everything.

My first group had Teddy in it. He was such a jerk with an indifferent attitude. He hated being there. He hated us, and he worked hard to let us know.

"What do you think?" Matt asked me about the lecture.

"Well, I know if you retain too much carbon dioxide in your system, you will go into respiratory acidosis," I replied.

"You think you know everything," Teddy taunted me. "Everybody worship me, for I am Alora Funk," he mocked.

"Just ignore him," Matt told me.

"Yeah, ignore me, Alora," Teddy said.

"Hey, at least Alora got in here because of her smarts. I heard you got in here because your daddy donated a wing to the library for your entrance fee. He paid over a million dollars to get his dopey, good-for-nothing son in," Matt jabbed back.

Teddy stood up and threw his chair to the ground, creating a loud bang in the study lounge. Good thing no one was around for us to disturb. He put his fists up. "You wanna fight?"

Matt stayed calm in his seat. "And get kicked out of Harvard for good? You aren't worth that."

"What, are you chicken?"

I was sick of Teddy. We all were. I would fight him but in my way. With my Zen, I grabbed some of Teddy's energy and gave it to Matt. Teddy didn't completely fall as Dr. Harrison had, but he stumbled to the floor. His head was rolling around, and he crawled up on all fours. He looked like a sick dog about to vomit. The color in his face drained.

I glanced at Matt. He hadn't even noticed Teddy because the extra energy enraptured him. He looked at his hands and then spun in a circle. His smile spread across his face. He ran in place.

"I feel great!" he said, entirely forgetting about Teddy. The other two girls in the group glanced back and forth between Matt and Teddy. They looked confused as they tried to figure things out. Matt acted like he was high on drugs, while Teddy seemed like he was dying on the floor. It was great. I loved learning more about what I could do with energy, and I loved watching Teddy suffer. He deserved the humiliation as he rocked on all fours. After Teddy wet himself, I gave him three-quarters of his energy back. I let Matt keep the last quarter since he had stood up for me. He deserved it.

With most of his energy returned, Teddy jumped and ran out of the lounge. He hadn't even bothered to grab his things. I hoped his disgracing experience would give him a slice of humility.

As we rotated study groups, I wanted to have more fun. I wasn't as greedy with the other's energy as I had been with Teddy's. I would grab little parts of someone's energy and pass it around the group, watching members instantly become tired while others rejuvenated. My fourth group was in the library, and every time the librarian passed our table, I would zap her with a bolt of energy. When it hit her, she would jump and let out a small squeak. I wondered if it felt like an electric shock. She would eye our table, not daring to go by it again. I couldn't believe how much I was learning and having the time of my life.

Monday, I couldn't wait to see Dr. Moody. At first, I was going to tell him about what had happened, but I decided to show him instead. I hadn't wanted to be rude and take his energy, so I gave him a minor hit of mine. It was a low hit because I didn't know how much he could handle. He continued eating, not even reacting to my small zap. I repeated it until I had hit him five times with it.

"Have you been feeling that?" I couldn't take the silence anymore.

"Feeling what," he said with a poker face.

"Have you been feeling bolts of energy?"

"Well, yeah. What do you know about that?" he asked, giving me a strange look.

I had a huge smile. "I have figured out how to control energy. I can grab it from people and objects and share it with others. I have been giving you some of my energy."

"Do it again," he challenged.

I hadn't touched the shrimp pasta he had prepared for us. Did I like shrimp? I looked at it and didn't want it to get cold, but realized I could just reheat it. "Do you mind if I take yours for a moment?" I asked.

"Only if you return it."

I reached out with my Zen and grabbed his energy, only a tiny amount. He went limp in his chair and instantly peed his pants. He looked sick, and it frightened me. I didn't think I had taken too much. Quickly, I returned it, scared of what I had done. He was obviously feebler than Dr. Harrison had been.

"Alora, did you mean for me to wet myself?"

I blushed and looked away.

"That was something else, though," he continued. "So you took my energy and returned it," he surmised as he looked down at his pants. "I'm going to have to run home and change," he said a matter of factly. I couldn't look at him in the eyes, knowing I had caused that.

"Yes, that was me."

"Did you do that to Dr. Harrison last Friday?" he asked.

I wouldn't answer him because I didn't want to get in trouble, but he already knew the answer. I took my eyes off my lap and said, "Yes, that was me."

Dr. Moody's hands covered his mouth, and he sort of laughed, coughed, with a wet rattle in his chest.

I smiled, proud of myself.

"Can you move things?" he asked.

I am not sure why, but I hadn't really tried. I had moved my pencil once, but then I had been distracted by taking object's energy forces. I suddenly had the desire to experiment more with telekinesis. But it wasn't really telekinesis. I didn't will something to move. I used energy to make it move.

Wanting to see if I could impress Dr. Moody more -and interested in what I could do-I used my Zen to take books off the shelf.

While the books were spinning, I evaporated his little accident so he could be comfortable. I had twelve off the shelf and began spinning them in a circle, somewhat like a tornado of books. We could feel their wind flow as they spun in orbit. Dr. Moody looked completely enraptured by my experiment, as was I, for not only could I do it, but it was easy for me. One by one, I returned the books to the shelf.

"Alora, that is phenomenal!" Dr. Moody had a fun look on his face, one I hadn't seen before. His eyes seemed to twinkle, reminding me of a toddler at a puppet show.

"Yeah, I guess so."

"Make me a promise," Dr. Moody said as he rubbed his long fingers together, a sound of sandpaper coming off them. He had such dry skin, that it almost looked like it would crack.

"Alright," I replied. I wondered what magnificent feat he wanted me to try.

"Have you told anyone about this yet?" he asked.

"No, I was waiting for you to be the first one I shared it with."

"That is very considerate of you. Please don't share this with anyone. At least not yet."

"But why? I really wanted to show Dr. Van Hassel."

"Please, trust me on this, Alora. I will give you a better answer tomorrow, but until then, don't tell anyone."

I promised Dr. Moody I wouldn't. After classes, I planned on spending the rest of the night experimenting with moving things. Was there a weight limit on what I could move? When I returned to my dorm, there was a letter from Peggy on my pillow. The letter made me forget about Telekinesis until my next meeting with Dr. Moody. It read:

Dear Alora,

I am so sorry for the way our parting went. Can you please forgive me? I now look back at it, and I am sure I looked really selfish in not letting you go to summer camp. Please let me explain my reasoning. I was so scared. It is as simple as that. I know it sounds like a poor excuse for not letting you go to camp. But, I was trying to protect you. You see, I had a best friend in ninth grade who went to summer camp. It is funny, because she begged and begged her mom to let her go. Her mom kept saying she had a bad feeling about it, but my friend begged so much, her mom finally let her go. I tried to get my parents to let me go, but when they said no, I didn't ask again. I wasn't that type of kid to go against their word. Anyway, my friend went to camp, and guess what? She came home pregnant. It was awful, for she wasn't that type of girl, but as you can see, anything can happen at camp, for kids aren't really supervised at camp. No one there holds an invested interest in the kids like their parents do.

I didn't want to put you in a situation where your virtues and values would be tested. Hillary said I needed to give you that chance so you would be strong. I guess she was right.

I know what a big deal this camp is going to be to your career. I have researched it while you have been there and I am blown away by what kind of things they have set up for you. I imagine you are going to come home a brainiac.

We sure miss you. I want you to know I have talked to Mr. Cox and he said we can take you back when you return, if you agree . I am so sorry I closed the door for a moment. I was angry and I had acted poorly.

The kids miss you. Mike misses you. I miss you. Please have fun, but please come back to us soon. And while you are there, remember who you are. Make good choices and stay away from boys.

Love,

Mom Sanibel.

...

It was as if Peggy's letter was a magic eraser that erased all the hurt she had caused me. I had been scared to leave camp when it ended because I didn't know where I was going to go. I missed the Sanibels a little, but I really missed everything else. I missed the reservoir and canyon. Maybe they would take me camping. I missed my school and Marge. I was excited to go back.

And yeah, maybe I missed Peggy.

I tried to fall asleep, but Sharon made too much noise, and she kept me awake. She cranked her radio up and jammed to it while studying. It was past midnight, and I started feeling sick from still being awake.

"Please turn the music off and go to bed," I whined for what felt like the hundredth time.

"Can't. This homework is due tomorrow. I can't let my grades slip."

"I can't go to sleep with all of your racket. At least turn your radio off," I yelled as I threw the pillow over my head.

"Hey, I didn't ask for you to be my roommate. My parents paid for a private dorm so I could stay up as late as I needed to in order to get my homework done."

"I need to sleep."

"My grade is worth more than your sleep," she said, turning the volume up a notch. Someone banged and yelled through the wall, "Shut up!"

"Yeah, Alora, shut that music off!" Sharon said as she put her mouth close to the wall.

She turned her volume down enough not to bother our neighbors anymore but still loud enough to prevent me from going to sleep. As I kept the pillow over my head, my anger grew. What a selfish person she was. All Sharon ever cared about was her advancement. She didn't care whose toes she crushed on the journey as long as she felt she got ahead. I didn't like the negative feelings I felt for her, but I couldn't help it. And then, it seemed like all the lights came on in my brain.

Sharon obviously has too much energy.

I could make her want to go to sleep in seconds. I sat up and watched her. This was going to be sic. I couldn't wait. Vengefully, I reached my Zen out and took some energy from her, as I had with Dr. Harrison. She collapsed to the floor, too weak to do anything but twitch. Maybe I had taken too much. I didn't want to kill her. I let her suffer for a few more seconds, then returned enough energy that she could sit up. She looked like a patient in the ICU with her pale skin and strange moans. Without brushing her teeth or putting her homework away, she crawled into her bed and slept. I hoped she hadn't wet herself.

I had absorbed her energy, and it made me hyper. No longer exhausted, I wanted to run around the room, feeling it surge through me as it visited every cell within. Since I was no longer tired, I wanted to crank the radio on and see how she liked it. It was too late to be so pumped up. I took a ball of my energy and sent it through the wall into the dorm on the other side. Happy to have Sharon asleep, I quickly joined her in the land of slumber.

In the morning, Sharon hadn't regenerated all of her energy back. She had thick, baggy eyes that looked like Mr. Cox usually had. It made a good experiment. Why hadn't her body been fully restored? She moaned a lot as she tried to finish her homework. Looking out the window, I had an idea as I watched students walk by. I started ciphering small bits of energy from each person down below. Since it was such tiny amounts, I doubted anyone would notice it was gone. I took the collection of energy and gave it to Sharon. I must have overdone it because she started jumping on her bed, simultaneously throwing her bedding onto the floor. She squealed like a four-year-old.

"It looks like someone woke up," I said.

"Yeah, it is the weirdest thing. Just moments ago, I was so tired I almost wondered if I was dying, but now I feel like I can move a mountain."

"Interesting. You almost thought you were dying. On a scale of one to ten, how tired were you?"

"A thousand."

"Hmm, interesting. Did you hurt?

"Yes and no. It hurt not to have energy, but it wasn't the same type of pain as if I had slammed my finger with a hammer."

"Why don't you use that energy and finish your homework assignment?"

"Oh, good idea!" she said.

I don't know why I helped her with her energy. She had been such a jerk the night before. She deserved to be sluggish and fail her assignment. But, I guess all the Sundays I had gone to church with the Sanibels had formed a bit of a consciousness in me. As I wanted to see Sharon suffer, I remembered Jesus Christ and how he had prayed for those who had hurt him.

Sharon finished her work the last fifteen minutes before we had to leave. "Wow, that was the fastest I ever got homework done," she said. "I'm so alert."

I couldn't hide my smile.

Chapter 9

I FOUND CLASSES DREADFULLY dull, like the professors were trying to teach the ABCs to someone with a double doctorate in English. Nothing new was being taught. Without thinking, I used my Zen and picked the paper off my desk. It looked like it was levitating. I had forgotten where I was. Nervous, I hurried and dropped it and looked around the room. No one paid any attention to me. The class looked hollow, like they were burnt out and about to fall asleep. What did Dr. Van Hassel expect when creating such a rigorous summer camp? Sure, we were geniuses, but we were also kids. We needed breaks. We needed socialization. We needed something more than days stacked on each other filled with lectures and homework. At least I didn't have to pay attention. When I was sure no one was watching me, I used my Zen to pick the paper off the table again. I tossed it back and forth, then dropped it.

I shot my hand up in the air. "Can I be excused to the bathroom?" I asked.

"Is it bathroom break right now on your agenda?" he asked condescendingly. Dr. Morris was a stickler for rules. He refused to do a thing that wasn't in correspondence to a rule.

"I would like to use my free pass," I said. We had all been given two bathroom passes to use whenever needed. Other than that, we were expected to go during the breaks on the agenda. Once the passes were gone, we were out of luck.

"I suppose if you want to squander your pass at this very moment, then I am not permitted to get in your way, but I would like to bring it to your attention how class excuses in ten minutes, and one would be wise to wait and use the pass on a more opportune time."

"Sorry, I must go now," I said as I jumped up and ran by his desk, tossing my pass at him. It missed his desk and fell on the floor.

"Hey, stop and pick this up," he hollered after me. I kept running.

I ducked into the bathroom and looked under all the stalls.

Alone.

I emptied the contents of my backpack on the counter.

"Okay, let's do this," I said. I picked each thing up with my Zen. I found that heavier items used more of my energy. Just like at Dr. Moody's office, I was open to multiple Zens and could lift many things simultaneously. I smiled as I watched the textbooks float around the bathroom. I had pens going in circles. I formed my papers into airplanes and had them zooming around the room. While the contents of my backpack were flying around the bathroom, I turned the water faucets on. I took the water with my Zen and splashed it across the wall. I lifted the water from the toilets into dancing, swirling water displays.

"I rule!" I exclaimed in a triumphant tone: me, the queen of the bathroom—the queen of energy manipulation.

The bathroom door opened. Instantly, I cut my Zen off, and everything fell to the floor. The bathroom looked trashed by my things. A pool of toilet water covered the tile. Maybe it would clean the mildew out of the grout.

"What are you doing in here?" a third-year student asked as she saw the mess.

"I tripped," I lied. "Did the bell ring?" I asked.

"Yeah, like five minutes ago."

I had been in the bathroom for fifteen minutes! Time had cruised. The third-year student went into a stall.

"Eww, the toilet seats are all wet, and so is the floor. What have you been doing?"

I used my Zen to levitate all my things back into my backpack quickly. I felt a little drowsy. I noticed I had depleted some of my energy with the bathroom party. As I left the bathroom, I stole a bit of the third-year student's energy to replenish my own, just a sliver so she could still function. I then caught up with my study group at our outside meeting spot.

I spent the rest of the day perfecting my Zen. The more I levitated things, the easier it had come to me. I think a few times, other students noticed the objects around the classroom floating. I had decided to lift things in the corners of the classroom, keeping the experiment far from me. That way, no one would connect it to me.

I couldn't wait to meet with Dr. Moody, but unfortunately, he was sick.

Such crappy timing. I want him to see what I can do.

It took such restraint not to flaunt my abilities. I kept it to myself because Dr. Moody had made me promise.

"I am just going to tell the others," I said to Dr. Moody, even though I was alone. "What does it matter?"

I took a little of Sharon's energy that night at the dorm. "I can't believe how tired I suddenly am. Just like last night. This isn't normal." As she climbed into bed, I hid my face under my pillow and laughed. It would teach her never to be a night owl again. I didn't know if it was a Christian thing to do, but I hadn't embraced Christianity. The next day, I worked on my abilities again in first and second period, and then I went outside with my group for study time.

Our study group had met outside next to a few trees. It didn't take long for our topic to get off subject, and soon, everyone talked about what superhero they would be.

"I would control people's minds," Dustin said.

"I would fly," Nate said.

"I would stop time," said Jerald.

"I would make fire," Steve said.

"What about you," Dustin asked me. "What would you do, Alora?"

"Um, fly, I guess."

I decided I already had superhero powers, for I could move things. The kids in the group continued to debate why their chosen power was better than everyone else's. Nate went on and on about what he would do if he could fly, which gave me an idea.

While they continued their pissing match, I reclined against a tree and looked like I might nap. Everyone ignored me, which was what I wanted.

It was time for fun.

I stretched my Zen forth, picked up Nate, and levitated him. Since he was heavier than anything I had experimented with, he used much more of my energy.

"Holy Toledo, Nate, you are flying! You are flying!" Jerald screamed.

"How are you doing that?" Steve asked, equally excited.

"I don't know, I don't know," Nate said in astonishment. I had him do aerial summersaults, spinning forward, then back. His brown hair flipping all around. The study group members stood with their eyes locked on Nate. He had an expression simultaneously of pure delight and utter fear. As I moved him around, I tried keeping him close to the ground. I could feel my energy sapping away. It took a lot to keep him in the air.

"Can you go higher?"

"How fast can you go?"

"Pick me up, and fly with me," the others said to him.

"So cool," I said as I stood up. Standing was hard to do, and I was tiring quickly. I borrowed a bit of Steve's energy to keep Nate up for a little bit longer. Nate tried to control the direction of his levitation, but I didn't allow that.

Despite Steve's added energy, I was getting weak. It had taken almost everything I had to fly Nate around, and I carefully dropped him to the ground. HE OWED ME since I had made his wish come true, so I borrowed some of his energy to restore my lost reserves. I still felt weak, so I also borrowed a little from Steve, Dustin, and Jerald.

The boys gathered around Nate. "How did you do that?"

"Do it again."

"Take me for a flight."

Our group didn't get any more studying in. When it was time, we went back to class. Word quickly spread across the campus about how Nate had flown, making him an instant celebrity. When kids asked me about it, I underplayed it.

"I am not sure he was really flying. I think it was an illusion the group had created," I told people. As the rumor circulated, some were willing to believe it, but most did not. My name never got tied up in the event.

I was happy to have Dr. Moody back in class on Monday. He invited me back to his office for dinner when class was dismissed. There was lime chicken with goat cheese and pine nuts in the middle. He was introducing me to fine food. "I always eat well. Life is too short not to." I could tell by his portly belly that he did. As he sat across from me, he had a twinkle in his eye. His aura was a golden orange.

"That was you, wasn't it?" he said.

I blushed and looked away. "I don't know what you are talking about."

"Making that boy fly. Tell me that had nothing to do with you."

I continued to look at the flower that graced our table. I sent my Zen to the flower and presented it to Dr. Moody. He reached out and grabbed it.

"I must say, I am very impressed."

"Thanks," I said, finally looking at him in the eyes.

"But I am also scared."

"Are you scared of the unknown?" I asked.

"I am scared for your future."

"I am sure my future is pretty bright," I replied.

"No, no, it is not. You must be careful, or you will have no future."

"What do you mean?"

"I want you to watch a movie. What do you have going the rest of the day?"

"Science engineering, break, then math."

"You are going to miss science engineering. Is that all right?"

"I thought I wasn't supposed to deviate from the agenda."

"You're not."

"Well, then, how am I going to do it?"

"I will tell them I detained you."

"Will I get in trouble?"

"I won't let you get in trouble," he said.

He didn't seem to be much in a hurry. I told him that watching the movie while we ate would save time, but he didn't want to. He said the film was disturbing and it would spoil our fine dinner. After we ate, he cleaned up his desk. We went into his classroom, where he put on a movie. I must admit it was a bit creepy sitting in the vast lecture hall alone with Dr. Moody.

I don't know why, but I had been expecting an entertaining movie. It wasn't. It wasn't even a professional documentary of any type. It was an electronic journal of sorts. A scientist created it. His focus was on a twelve-year-old girl. It was old, recorded many years before. The guy in the movie explained in scientific jargon, which I fully understood, how the girl had telekinetic abilities. He took to calling the girl subject 341, depersonalizing her.

The camera focused on subject 341. She was in a small, cement room. She could levitate paper and magnets and playing cards. He tried to have her do bigger things, but at first, she couldn't do it. Seeing her in the cement room made me wonder if I was ever subjected to the same experiments.

Each time he recorded her, she was able to lift bigger objects. By the end, she had been able to lift a chair for a short distance across the room. Although the movie had been painfully long, it had ended without any conclusion.

"I don't see how it was disturbing," I said.

"I'm sure it didn't look disturbing, but the story behind the movie is this -Dr. Granger had found this girl. I believe she had been on a local news channel when someone had reported to them what she could do. Anyhow, this girl's name was Candice Clemmings. I researched as much about her as I could.

"Candice was a ward of the state. That means the state-owned her in a sense. She didn't have parents. In nineteen seventy-four, she lived at an Orphanage in Chicago called *Angel Guardian*. The state was in the process of shutting down the orphanage. They had hundreds of kids to get rid of. When Dr. Granger requested Candice Clemmings, they easily released her custody to his university."

"What university was it? This one?"

"Oh no, Harvard would never get itself involved in a scandal like that one."

"What university was it then?"

"I am not going to say, for I am embarrassed by what they did, and I currently have several friends working there. I don't want to tarnish their name."

"Are you sure it wasn't Harvard?" I asked.

"I promise on my mother's grave," he said sternly.

"So, what happened? Why is this a bad story? It sounds like they rescued Candice. I am much like her. I liked it when I was rescued."

"The fact you are like her scares me even more. I don't think Candice had the same abilities you do. Somehow, she had broken into the science of telekinesis, but I think that is where her gifts started and stopped. Anyway, Dr. Granger subjected that poor child into tests, upon tests, upon tests. When he wasn't testing her, he was forcing her to entertain colleagues with her telekinetic abilities.

"He drained the life out of this poor child. She never got a break, for he was going insane. He thought he had discovered a scientific breakthrough and wasn't about to miss his opportunity to have his name written up in all the scientific journals.

"Candice Clemmings slowly lost the ability for telekinesis. I think he had overworked her. As he saw it slip away, he saw his dreams go with it. He wouldn't let it happen, so he mixed up a drug cocktail and gave it to her. Her abilities sprouted during that time. Do you remember in the movie when she moved the chair? She had done that after he had given her all those drugs. He got greedy and kept giving her stronger doses. Her teeth quickly rotted, and her hair fell out. In the end, it took her life."

I felt sick. I really wished Dr. Moody hadn't shared her story with me. I guess it was good that we had finished our dinner. "Why didn't anyone stop him? Why was he allowed to do that to a kid?"

"I guess it was because Candice Clemmings didn't have anyone to watch over her, to advocate for her. None of Dr. Granger's colleagues knew the extent of what was going on. They all testified they thought subject 341's mom was dropping her off at the university every now and then. They didn't realize Dr. Granger locked her in his lab like a lab monkey."

Rage filled me for Dr. Granger, and I don't know why, but I was angry at Dr. Moody for telling me all this. "That is so disturbing. Why did you have to tell it to me?"

"Because, Alora Funk, I don't want to see you become the next Candice Clemmings."

"What do you mean?" I asked.

"I see this happening all over again. You are a ward of the state, aren't you? You don't have any parents or anyone who cares about you, watching over you."

His words hurt.

"It's already happening. The state let you come to Harvard for a month. One full month of no supervision. Have they checked in with you?"

I shook my head.

"No, I didn't think so. We could have already zapped your brain by now. You are light years ahead of Candice Clemmings. You already have the heads of all the departments spinning with your abilities of recollection and recall. The last thing they need to know is how you can channel object's energy, and you can lift things with that energy."

"They wouldn't do anything to me. Things have changed a lot since the seventies," I naively said.

"You really think so? Alora, my dear, this has already happened to you. You have already been the guinea pig to someone."

"Who, you?" I asked.

"Oh, heavens no, not me. To the Russians, whoever they represented. You told me you were locked in a cement room and imprisoned by a drug-induced coma. They didn't do that to you because they wanted a vegetable in the basement. They were doing some experimentation on you; you mark my word. This is very real, and the potential of you ending up like Candice Clemmings is very real."

I felt horrible. I wanted to run and hide. I wanted to give back all my weird gifts and be like everyone else. I wanted to become lost in the hustle and bustle of the Sanibel family.

"What am I supposed to do?" I glumly asked.

"I don't know, lay low, I guess. Don't appear to be so brilliant. Whatever you do, do not let anyone run experiments on you. They will start out small; ask if they can hook up an electrode to your brain to measure your neurological brain activity, but don't let them. Once they start, there will be more tests, and they will keep going and never end. Just don't allow them to test you."

"But they test me all the time," I said.

"How so?"

"I don't know, like all the tests we do every Monday."

Dr. Moody laughed. "No, those are fine. You can take academic tests on paper but nothing else, do you promise?"

"I promise. I still don't know what I am supposed to do."

"I don't know. Enjoy that you are brilliant, and get a nice career with it, but nothing else. Don't be experimented upon, and don't show off. If you start letting people know you can pick up objects with your own energy, they will lock you up against your will. I promise you that."

"Can I always turn to you if I need to?" I asked.

"Of course, you can," he said, giving me a one-armed, friendly hug from the side.

I went back to my dorm very depressed. I had been having fun with my new abilities, but now I didn't want them, for they scared me.

⸺⸺◦⸺⸺

SHARON WAS PARTICULARLY sour. She had received a correspondence in the mail from her family, with five hundred dollars crisply tucked in the card.

"I am not allowed to leave the campus. You guys should have known that. What good is these five hundred dollars if not to torture me? I hate it here. I want to get out for one night, but is that too much to ask? Why are they so controlling? This is our lives, not theirs!"

I was lying in bed, and she kept going on and on. I couldn't take any more of it. I opened my Zen and was going to use it, but I held back for a moment.

Is it wise to keep messing with someone's energy? What are the long-term consequences? I really had no idea what the physical effects on the body were.

"I think I would call a taxi and sneak out if I didn't have such an idiotic roommate. That is why I needed my own dorm. Why did they stick me with such a loser?"

Did she think I was asleep, or was she hoping I was awake? Either way, her words stung.

She sat on her bed and combed out her frizzy orange hair. I took some of the static electricity from her brush and zapped her butt with it.

"Ouch," she said, jumping up.

She saw my letter from Peggy, picked it up, and mocked everything on it. "Alora, you better not go home from camp pregnant. Peggy won't like that. She doesn't have to worry about that. No boy would date you." She looked over more of the letter. "Mike misses you. Oh, poor Mike. What is he doing with you so far away?"

She ripped up my letter and picked hers back up. I had all I could take.

Still pretending to be asleep, I sent my Zen to her and ignited the five hundred dollars in her hand. Instantaneously, it went up in smoke.

"Ahh," Sharon screamed, dropping the flaming money on her bed. The fire spread over her homework and her quilt. She screamed again as she opened her water bottle and tried to put the flames out. The smoke billowed to the fire alarm, and it went off like an ear-piercing siren. The sprinkler heads popped out, and the floodgates opened. I sat up in bed as if I had woken up to the siren.

"What's going on?" I asked, rubbing my eyes.

———————⬥———————

OUR DORM WAS EVACUATED even though the sprinklers put out the small fire before the firefighters arrived. The water had damaged our side of the dorms, displacing us and the other eight girls in the program. They sent us to another dorm. Sharon was suspended for arson since it was against policy to have any flammables or fire paraphernalia in the room.

I had to admit I felt slightly bad and responsible for her punishment. The damage was going to be costly. They promised Sharon if her parents covered the cost of the restoration, then she would be allowed to return the following year.

To my luck, I had my new dorm to myself.

The next evening, as I dined on lobster tail with Dr. Moody, he finally brought up the subject of the fire.

"Was that you?" he asked.

Why did he always think everything was me? I couldn't look him in the eyes as I felt my cheeks flush.

"How was it me?"

"I read the reports. Sharon claimed the whole time that the money had spontaneously combusted. No person on the faculty believes her, except maybe me, considering who her roommate was."

"Who, me?"

"Did you know she is in a lot of trouble? Are you okay with her taking the brunt of what should be *your* punishment?"

"I didn't mean to. Should I go and tell Dr. Van Hassel it was me?"

"NO! What's done is done," he snapped as he dipped a chunk of red lobster meat into a ceramic bowl of melted butter. I hadn't eaten lobster before, so I mimicked his actions. My first bite blew me away. The rich, buttery goodness of the meat was astounding. I never knew food could taste so good. I loved the education into refinement that Dr. Moody gave me.

"Do you think her parents will pay for the damage?" I asked with my cheeks stuffed full of potatoes.

"They won't be happy about it, but most kids in this summer camp have parents with pretty deep pockets. That Sharon kid was a bit of a tort, and I reckon she will return more humble next year."

We ate for a moment in silence.

"How did you do it?" Dr. Moody asked.

"Do what?"

"Start fire?"

"My energy got so hot it combusted."

"Precisely what I thought happened. Can you do it again?"

"Is this an experiment?" I joked.

"You don't have to do it if you are uncomfortable."

"Will you put it out before it sets the sprinklers off?" I asked. "I can't be connected to two fires on the campus."

"How about we go to my lab?" he said.

I followed him into the lab. He put a dry piece of parchment on a worktable. "Go ahead," he said.

I pulled my Zen out and worked myself up until I felt it scorching, then sent it to the parchment. The paper went up in flames. I felt powerful watching what I had done. Quickly, he covered it with a metal lid before too much smoke appeared.

"You are a rare treasure."

I beamed.

———— ◉ ————

OVER THE WEEKEND, I used my study time to experiment more on my findings. I could move things, to transfer energy, and to create fire. I had to be careful with the fire.

I can't set off any more sprinklers. So, I pretty much left it alone.

Since I had the dorm room to myself, I rearranged all my furniture with my Zen. When I was done, I felt depleted of my energy. I looked out the window to see if there was anyone I could borrow some energy from, but no one walked by. I reached through the walls and grabbed some from the girls on the other side.

———— ◉ ————

"THE THING IS," I TOLD Dr. Moody over bacon-potato chowder. "I get so warn-out when I move things. I have to use my energy to do it. Then I become pretty weak."

"Why do you have to use your energy?" he asked.

"Well, it is done with energy. It has to come from somewhere."

"Why don't you take from the energy around you? I know I don't have to tell you this, for you already know it, but there is energy everywhere. We live in giant energy fields. Tap into these fields and use them for your energy of transference."

"You are brilliant," I shouted.

Why hadn't I thought of that first?

I started tapping into the energy from all around. I felt blown away by the massive amount of available energy around us. Here, we lived in a world always crying about insufficient energy, and it was right here!

As I used the free energy source, my movements with the objects became smoother and more refined. The great thing was I didn't tire when I borrowed from the abundant energy all around. The other thing I liked was whenever I got tired, I would reenergize myself with the energy field. I used to feel a little evil when I would take energy from others to rebuild my own.

The next day, when I was playing with energy fields, I made the discovery of a lifetime.

I could use my Zen and feel the molecules in objects I touched. Since I had the chemical composition of literally every element recorded in my memory, I could experiment with molecular composition. I was glad Dr. Moody had let me memorize his books. With that knowledge, I rearranged the matter in my homework paper and turned it into a rock. It wasn't difficult because we are surrounded by all the molecules needed to create things. They are right there, abundantly available. It is like everything around us is waiting to be formed and manipulated.

I had done this at the Sanibel's, but I hadn't known how. Now I did.

Weirdly, no one else can do this. What a different world this would be if we all had this ability.

I added what I needed to the paper to create the rock.

I transformed a leaf into grass and grass into a leaf during my study group. I changed water into ice. I turned my socks into pillows and even took a short nap on them. My experiments were so small and secret no one noticed what I was up to. I couldn't wait to see Dr. Moody.

———⊙———

"OH MY, OH MY, OH MY," Dr. Moody said, as he watched me rearrange the matter in his plate and make it become a *teapot*. "It is good you are leaving here soon, kid."

"Why?" I asked, a little hurt.

"Because if you stay around much longer, I might start experimenting on you myself." I laughed at what he said, but I think he must have meant it because he wouldn't allow us to have dinner together anymore. The next time after class, he dismissed us and immediately locked himself in his office.

"Why can't I come in?" I asked, pounding on his door.

"Because you are too much of a temptation."

"Temptation? Temptation for what?"

"You have the abilities to change this whole world. You have a power beyond anything comprehendible. You are what all scientists search for."

"Then help me channel it. Help me know what to do with it."

Dr. Moody cracked his door open. "Only you can do that."

"But I don't know what to do with it."

"Alora, not only do you have an amazing ability, but you also have all the scientific knowledge to go along with it. At least you are not an idiot who has been given this ability. That could be very dangerous. You have a brilliant mind and will figure out how to best channel your abilities. I warn you. Be very careful who you share your secret with, for even your own mother, if you had one, might betray you to tap into your power. So please, keep most of this to yourself. Don't let yourself fall into the wrong hands, for your abilities could destroy the world."

"Please help me?" I begged. The fear inside me seemed crippling.

Dr. Moody slammed the door so fast. He almost got my nose in it. "I am sorry," I heard him through the door. "You hold so much potential. You are now a temptation to me. You shouldn't have shared this knowledge with me. For now, I want to test your abilities. I want to experiment upon you and have my name written up in the scientific journals."

"I trust you. I don't mind. You can experiment upon me. I will let you," I said. The way he hid from me severed my spirit. I was desperate to keep our friendship going. I would have done anything for him.

He squeaked the door open again. "Please, Alora, don't be so naive. You can't trust anyone, not even me," he slammed the door again.

"But I will let you experiment with me. I, too, want to know my capacity, like you do. You can help me run tests and things so we can know my full potential. I don't think I could do this on my own." Warm tears slid down my cheeks. At least I would have some fun with them. By the time they dripped into my hands, I had changed them into bright skittles.

I popped them into my mouth.

The door flew open, and a cup of water splashed into my face. "LEAVE!" he screamed.

I ran bawling from his classroom. He broke my heart into a million pieces.

Chapter 10

OUR LAST DAY OF CAMP was Saturday, and the university threw us a goodbye banquet. They included students from all years. Embarrassingly, I won all three awards for the first-year class.

When I returned to my dorm room for my last night, there was a letter on my bed. It was from Mr. Cox.

Alora,

I wanted to inform you that you have two families who
wish to foster you. I do not wish to influence you
in any way, but I want you to consider your
best option. The first family is the Sanibels. They
are sorry for kicking you out and wish for your return. I want
you to remember they did kick you out.
They are a fine family, I suppose, but
they probably will never adopt you.
The second family is the Petersons. They live in a two-bedroom
Apartment in Ogden City. It is way bigger than Mantua.
They want to adopt you if that is what you
want. You would likely find
a lovely home with them. They are a young couple without kids.
Please let us know your decision when
you arrive back to Utah. I will
be at the airport to pick you up.
Mr. Cox

Suddenly, I felt terrible for calling Mr. Cox Mr. Scary for so long. It was because of him I made it to camp. Maybe he would turn out to be my only true friend.

Or perhaps Alora Funk was not meant to have friends.

I DIDN'T SLEEP, BECAUSE I had too much to think about. Who would I return to live with? Both of the families had potential, but there were also negatives to both.

With the Sanibels, I would have a large family. I would live in their unique yellow house by the reservoir. I loved the reservoir. I loved the campground near their home and being in the canyon; however, I hated the messes. I hated being hungry. I hated how disconnected the Sanibels were with the kids. I liked the shed and sleeping in it. I liked Athena. I wanted the freedom to come and go as I pleased.

With the Petersons, I might like not having siblings. I was sure if I needed clothes, they would buy some for me; however, I had a nice collection from Dr. Van Hassel. Erin had taken them to the dry cleaner earlier and packed them in the new luggage she had bought. Also, with the Petersons, I would get enough to eat. I wouldn't have to fight for my food. But I would hate living in an apartment in a city.

I couldn't make a choice. There were pros and cons to both decisions. When the sun rose, I was so tired from not sleeping. I felt foolish. Why had I allowed myself to become so tired? I gathered some energy and felt like I had a whole night's sleep and a healthy breakfast. I should sell my energy to tired college students. '*Safe energy for cheap*'. I would make a fortune.

Carlson came to my dorm and carried my two luggage bags to the limousine. I was glad to be leaving. Summer was almost over, and I wanted some free time before I found myself back in a classroom. But what would Box Elder Middle School have to offer? Harvard summer camp bored me, so a middle school would surely be like being stuck in a hell, lacking mental stimulation. Would the kids at school like my new clothes, or still find reasons to tease me about them? Honestly, they looked like old lady clothes shrunk and put on a teenager.

I climbed into Dr. Van Hassel's limo.

"I take it you had a lovely time here?" he asked.

"Oh yes, I did. Thanks for everything." I realized I hadn't seen much of him over the month.

"You earned it, so don't thank me. It came from a scholarship." He looked so prestigious in his black suit, vest, dark gray tie, and white, crisp shirt. I was glad I had the chance to rub shoulders with someone so important personally.

"I heard you gave me the scholarship and clothes," I said. Dr. Van Hassel's face became red. The mood turned uncomfortable as he looked away.

I decided to change the subject quickly.

"Do I get to come back next year?" I already knew I did. Of course, I never planned to return. I didn't want to waste another summer like that. I might consider it if Dr. Moody still was my friend.

"You know you do. But Alora, I have an offer even better than that."

"What is it?" I asked as I sipped the grape soda he had offered me. After a month of eating off Chinaware, I didn't want to go back to the Sanibel's crappy cups that made all the water taste like plastic. The limo went over a bump, and the purple liquid from my cup went on his white seat. My heart dropped into my stomach. He had been looking out the side of his window. He hadn't seen what I had done. Quickly, I slid my body over the purple stain so he wouldn't notice it.

Sitting over it, I used my Zen to remove the stain from the leather. I lifted my thigh and snuck a peak underneath—no more purple. I loved my Zen!

Dr. Van Hassel turned to me as he sat up tall. "Alora, we expected great things from you when you came this summer. Your abilities blew us away. I don't even think you realized what you were capable of."

Little does he know.

"You have managed to use your brain to a level none of the rest of us can hope to aspire to. It would be a shame to watch nothing happen with your gift. You must not let it go idle. I propose that you return to the school this fall, and we will tap into your potential."

I choked on some soda, coughing until I could clear my lungs. "What kind of tests?" I blurted out.

"Similar to the ones you already took. What we are looking to do is place you. If you are good enough, we can put you in accelerated programs and work toward your doctorate."

"You mean I could get a doctorate without taking any more classes?"

"Well, yes, and no. You could test out of some classes, but we don't intend to let your mind go idle. We would still like to see you learn."

"But what if I don't have anything left to learn? What if I know it all?"

"You are certainly pompous."

His remark cut into me, and I felt silly for my statement.

"Sure, there are always new things to learn. I imagine, and I could be wrong, you are well versed in the sciences, but what about other areas of life? Do you have a good grasp of history? Could you write a haiku? How are your grammar skills and English skills?

"I don't know. Why don't you ask me a question, and we will see if I know the answer," I responded.

"What is the Defense of the Realm Act, and when was it implemented?"

My mind was blank. "I don't know," I admitted.

"How about, what happened July first, nineteen sixteen?"

"Don't know."

"Just as I thought. You see, Alora, you still have a lot to learn."

⁂

DURING MY FLIGHT HOME, my mind raced. I had so many choices to consider, like where I would live. Did I want to return to Harvard in the fall? Did I really want to kiss away my childhood by spending the remainder of it in college? The last few weeks of the camp had dragged. If I returned in the fall, there wouldn't be kids my age. I wanted the experience of getting my driver's license and then cruising around places with friends. I wanted to go to parties, dances, and everything the Sanibel kids talked about. I would have my whole life to be an adult. I had only one childhood, most of which had already been stolen.

Of course, I was also afraid to return to Harvard. What if Dr. Moody was right? What if they wanted to run experiments on me? What if they hurt me or, zapped my brain, or filled me with drugs?

Would I like the Petersons? Would I miss siblings? I know I would miss the reservoir. We had driven to Ogden once, and it seemed like a scary place with lots of people and cars—nothing like Manua.

I loved where the Sanibels lived and even liked them a bit, but they weren't the greatest family. Although they boasted about how amazing they were, they really weren't.

What to do.

———◉———

MR. COX MET ME AT THE airport and took me back in his black car. I told him a little about the camp. I also told him about Dr. Van Hassel's offer. When he heard that, he became adamant I returned to Harvard in the fall. He said one in a million foster kids get a chance like that, and I would be an idiot if I turned it down.

Back at Child Protective Services, I sat in an empty room as Mr. Cox awaited my decision. He said he would call whatever family I chose, and they would be there shortly to pick me up.

"Don't put too much stress into figuring it out. You will only be there for two weeks before you have to return to Harvard."

Who said I was returning to Harvard?

The decisions weighed heavily upon me.

———◉———

THE LACK OF WELCOME crushed my heart like a giant anvil squeezing it to a popping point. For some reason, I had gotten it in my mind that the Sanibels had missed me. When I entered the living room, Mrs. Sanibel sat in her recliner, eating a big bag of chips while watching a movie on TV. The other kids ran around the house, like usual. The place seemed extra dirty and smaller than I had remembered. The scent of something rotten made me want to run back to Mr. Cox and ask for the Petersons.

Mike was the only one who had come and picked me up from Child Protective Services. The drive home had been painfully quiet. I tried to tell him a little about camp, but when it became apparent he wasn't listening, I stopped talking.

Mrs. Sanibel looked up from her chips as she wiped her greasy hands on the chair's upholstery. "Mercy me, you missed dinner. Don't worry, I didn't get enough to eat either." She took her hands and licked the salt off them. Then she dived them back into the crinkly bag. She grabbed another handful of chips, shoved them into her mouth, and then held the bag to me.

"You can have a chip if you want."

My stomach turned as I imagined her slimy hands swimming through the other chips and making them soggy.

"I am fine," I said, which was a lie. I left for the airport before breakfast. I didn't have money to buy anything on the flight. When Mr. Cox picked me up, he hadn't stopped to think I might be hungry. I hadn't eaten all day.

"There might be some bread in the kitchen," she said in between licking her fingers.

The sadness felt like a monster, filling me with regret and disappointment. Peggy could have said hello. She didn't say, "Oh Alora, I am so glad you chose to come and live with us. You know how much we were missing you. I understand you could have gone and lived with that nice Peterson family where you never would be hungry and where everything is nice and clean, but you chose us instead, and I am so touched and honored by that." She never said that or anything to me.

Disappointed, I dragged my heavy luggage up the stairs. With each step I took, the luggage banged against the steps and wall. After three steps up, Mike came storming out of his room. "Who is making all that racket? It has to stop now!"

He looked up and saw me trying to get my luggage up the stairs. I expected an offer to carry my bags for me. Instead, he said, "Try to be more careful! Watch my walls!"

What jerks, the both of them. Why had I chosen to come back to the Sanibels? I wanted to bawl. My stomach growled at me, reminding me it was empty. I was so angry. I looked over at Peggy, whose attention had returned to some rambling commercial. I hated her at that moment. With my anger, I sent my Zen out and, grabbed her chip bag and dumped its crumbly contents all over her head. She snapped out of her TV trance and screamed. The bag landed in her lap. She picked it up with the tips of her fingers as if she thought it was possessed by evil spirits. She chucked the bag to the side of her chair. I laughed at all the chip pieces trapped in her frizz.

"Mercy me, how did it happen?" she jumped up, and the chips scattered even deeper into the chair and onto the floor. "No, no, no," she bellowed.

Mike came storming out of the room. "Ugh! What's with all the noise tonight?" He looked at Peggy as she danced around and spread her chip mess everywhere. "What are you doing? What is with your mess? I bet you are going to leave it there, huh? I bet you won't get off your fat butt long enough to clean it." What was he talking about, fat butt? His was even wider than hers. He never cleaned anything, so how could he justify being critical of her? Satisfied with the chip disaster, I continued dragging my luggage upstairs, taking extra care to bang them as loudly as possible.

"My walls, my walls," he turned and screamed at me.

Upstairs, I noticed Alashia and Emma had moved their things into my room. They were both on the floor playing dolls. They looked up at me, and both groaned.

"I'm not giving my room back," Alashia said.

"Me neither," said Emma.

-Another blow to me. I stared at all the trash in my room. They had put a bed on top of mine, creating a bunk bed. Another dresser had been put in. All of the girl's clothes and toys created a mountain of mess. Why had I come back? I thought about the nice, tidy room I would have at the Petersons. I turned from the girls and lugged my bags back down the stairs. It immediately sent Mike flying out of his room again.

"My walls, my walls!"

I was so tired. I wanted to curl up on the stairs and cry like a baby.

"If you put a hole in my wall, you will be fixing it," he threatened. He could have been a gentleman and offered to carry my bags.

I had enough. I didn't have to be tired, and Mike didn't have to be yelling. I could solve both of those problems in one quick move. I sent out my Zen, took his energy, and added it to mine. Instantly, I felt happy, despite the situation at the moment. I looked at Mike. He had lowered to the floor and sat against the wall. His face had a green tint to it.

"I don't feel good," he groaned. He looked pale. I finished dragging my luggage down the stairs and deliberately wheeled them over his outstretched toe as I went by him. "Watch it," he moaned, lacking the strength to yell.

Peggy never even looked up to ask me where I was going. I know she must have seen me out of her peripheral vision. I dragged my bags out onto the porch. I went back into the house and found the phone. I tried calling Mr. Cox to come and get me, but there was no answer. I even tried calling Marge, but there was no answer. What was I going to do? I had made a bad choice and didn't want to live there. I wanted to leave right that minute.

My stomach growled at me again. I wheeled my luggage to the shed and opened the outside freezer to find no fish in it, empty except for a thick layer of ice buildup.

Dang. I had planned on eating fish.

I decided to get the bread Peggy had mentioned. I walked back into the house, down the hall, past the dining room, through the family room, and into the kitchen. A bread bag on the floor with both ends ripped open and a few slices still inside, but they were dry and crusty. In desperation, I grabbed them. I looked around to see if there was anything else to eat, but there wasn't. I took the bread back to the shed with me.

I took a bite, and the dryness almost shut my throat down. I wish I had grabbed some water on the way out. I thought about returning to the house to get water but didn't want to go by the Sanibels again. As I debated going back, a thought hit me. I should make water. There was hydrogen and oxygen in the air all around me.

I would first need something to put it in. I looked to see if there were any cups in the shed. There weren't. I saw an old milk jug out there. That would work. I grabbed the milk jug with my Zen and rearranged the molecules until I had crafted a 16oz cup. I gathered the hydrogen and oxygen in the air and filled my cup with fresh water. I wasn't sure how it would taste. I took a drink and found the water refreshing, as it had no chemicals. I took a bite of the stale bread when another thought hit me. Why didn't I turn the bread into something worth eating? What was I in the mood for?

I held the bread in my left hand while using my Zen to gather all the needed elements. Since I had studied Dr. Moody's books, I knew the molecule makeup of almost everything out there. With my knowledge, I borrowed from the elements around me and constructed the atoms into a chicken. I took more of the milk jug and turned it into a plate. I put the chicken on it, then decided mashed potatoes would complement the meal nicely. I turned the other piece of bread into creamy potatoes. Things were a bit cool, so I used my energy and heated everything. My meal tasted amazing, and pride popped out of me like a firework show. If I could make food whenever I was hungry, maybe life at the Sanibels wouldn't be bad. When I was halfway done eating, Peggy came into the shed.

"You wanna take the boat out?" she asked. She saw my dinner, and I watched her salivate. "Where did you get that?" she asked.

"At the airport," I lied.

"Oh, looks good," she said, licking her lips. There was no way I was going to share with her. I watched her hook the boat trailer up to the four-wheeler. I had to suppress my laugh because I could still see little slivers of chips embedded into her hair.

⟶⟵

LIFE FELT PERFECT OUT on the water. All my stress melted away. A calmness filled me as I returned to my most favorite place. The heat from the scorching day lingered above. A cool breeze blew over, and then it felt perfect. Athena panted at my feet. I had my pole in my hand and a worm in the other. I wasn't in the mood for getting worm guts under my nails. When Peggy wasn't looking, I used my Zen to break the worm apart and put it on my hook. It was so great not touching the nasty worm with my fingers. After my line was cast, I could relax. I looked up at the brilliant white stars illuminating the dark sky. At that moment, everything was perfect. I was glad I had returned.

"Did you have a good time?" Peggy asked.

"Yes," I said.

"Are you as brilliant as they had hoped?"

I was dying to tell her all about the camp, from start to finish. I wanted to tell her about Dr. Moody and our dinners together. I wanted to tell her how I could control elements and manipulate energy, but I didn't trust her. I lost my trust for her the day she kicked me out. It still hurt me that she had easily turned her back to me. I had put up a wall against her, and I wasn't ready to take it down any time soon.

"I don't think I would call myself brilliant," I responded, even though I knew I was.

"Sure you are. I Googled their camp. Only twenty kids are picked out of thousands of applicants, and to think, you didn't even have to apply."

A bat dived bombed us, then zigzagged away. "Well, tell me all about your summer camp, and don't leave one detail out."

I pulled the crumpled-up agenda out of my pocket. I had memorized it, but I kept it close to me as a remembrance of my experience there. I handed the schedule to Peggy.

"What is this?" she asked.

"It was my daily agenda."

"Well, it's too dark out here to read it," she said, handing it back to me.

"Try again. Hold it up to the lantern." I replied.

She put it next to the lantern and read it. "Wow. That looks like a grueling way to spend a summer, worse than school. I hope you were happy there, and it was worth it to you."

"It was nice," I said, underplaying the whole thing.

"Well, tell me more. Who was your favorite teacher? Was it hard? You better not tell me you made a boyfriend there."

I kept my description short. I didn't want to tell her about any of my discoveries. Peggy couldn't be trusted. I kept it simple and very superficial. I told her the classes were challenging, and the tests were even more demanding.

"How did you do?" she asked. "I remember not very long ago, you couldn't even take a test." I laughed at what she said, and she laughed at me.

"I must have done well enough because they invited me to return there this fall."

"What about your eighth-grade year? Don't they realize you will be in school?"

"They want to graduate me with a doctorate in science. They said they would help me focus on one which builds my strengths, in return, they want me to join their research team and help them."

"You, the girl who couldn't speak a few months ago? What happened, Alora? Who are you?"

I felt nervous. Had I already told Peggy too much?

Chapter 11

WHEN WE PUT THE BOAT back in the shed, Peggy noticed my luggage out there.

"I thought I remembered you taking that upstairs and Mike yelling at you for it. What is it doing out here?" she asked.

"Alashia and Emma took over my room, so I came out here."

"They can't kick you out. Don't worry, there is room for you. Emma and Alashia can sleep together on the top bunk, and I will put you in the lower bunk."

"I thought foster kids were supposed to have their own rooms?" I reminded her.

"It's a technicality, dear. If they ever ask, tell them you do."

Peggy reached for one of my bags. "Let me help you in," she generously offered.

I grabbed the bag from her. "I am fine. I think I will sleep out here."

"Why would you want to do that?"

"Because it is nice out here."

"Where would you sleep?"

"On the cot."

"What cot?"

I looked at the cot next to the four-wheeler. Peggy parked the four-wheeler next to the cot every time she returned it.

"I didn't know we had a cot," she said.

She knew she did. She had woken me up on it many Sundays, but I wasn't about to argue.

"Don't be silly. There is plenty of space in your room for the three of you."

"Please, I actually like it out here."

"Well, if you don't mind. This can be your room until you start back to school. Oh, I guess unless you go to Harvard, then it is your room until you leave. Don't tell Child Protective Services about it. Deal?"

"Deal."

"Come on, Athena," Peggy said as she left the storage shed.

"Can you leave her out here?" I asked.

Peggy bent down and baby-talked Athena. "You wanna stay with Alora, huh? You want to stay outside?" Peggy let Athena give her a sloppy kiss on the lips.

After Peggy left, I remembered how hungry I was and took one of the fish I had caught and added heat to it from my Zen. Within seconds, it was hot and ready to eat. I put it on my homemade plate and had a lovely meal.

As I lay on my cot, I was glad for my choice. The family still had problems, but I hadn't necessarily returned for them. I had returned for Mantua. I had returned from the nightly fishing trips. I had returned for the nature and outdoors. I was kind of glad the girls had taken my room. I liked being in the shed so much better than their toxically dirty house.

The following day, I slept in because I had been so tired. When I went into the house, I found I had missed breakfast. I looked around and found a half-eaten pancake on somebody's plate. I took the plate and pancake out to the shed. With my Zen, I turned it into scrambled eggs, ham, and cheese. It was so good.

I tried to stick around the house to see if anyone had missed me or wanted to hang out. No one did.

"Give me that back."

"I don't have to. It's mine."

"No, it's mine." They seemed so more interested in fighting than in noticing me. It wasn't until Tuesday, when Corbon heard about my camp, he said, "You were gone for a whole month? No way, I don't believe you. You have been here this whole summer." -another hurtful comment from a Sanibel. Had no one noticed my absence?

I joined the dinner battle as we pushed and prodded for a scoop or two of casserole. My anger made me aggressive, and I rammed my shoulders and pushed the others and ended up with two full scoops on my plate. I sat down and guarded my plate as I debated if I should bring up what was on my mind.

Dinner time seemed like the only chance for an entire family conversation. For the first time, I had something to talk about. I took three bites of dinner, then said, "I would like for the family to go camping."

My emotions played games on me at all moments since I had returned, telling me that I should have gone to the Petersons. If I could get the family camping, then perhaps I wouldn't hate myself so hard for my decision to return.

"That is so much work to drag the family through the mountains." Had Peggy said that?

"There is a campground right in Mantua," I said.

"That's news to me," she responded. The next fifteen minutes turned into a debate between the family about whether a campground existed.

"I know for a fact there isn't one," Peggy stated abruptly.

"You willing to bet on it?" Corbon asked.

"Sure, what's the ante?"

"If I am right and there is one, then you take us camping next weekend," he said.

Whoopee! He is on my team.

"And if I am right and there isn't one, you clean the house for a week," Peggy said.

"Deal," Corbon replied. I took the last bite of my food, surprised that no one had stolen it from my plate. We were going camping! I punched the air, then buried my hand in my lap in embarrassment from the stares.

After dinner, the family decided to drive to the campground to see who the winner would be. Corbon and I won.

That night, Peggy and I went out on the boat. We didn't catch many fish, and I talked very little. I sat in the boat with a fraudster, a woman who told the world how wonderful she was, yet she was the most selfish person ever. I missed when I trusted her and could say to her things.

When we went fishing the next night, I decided to catch at least ten fish. At summer camp, I had heard one of the boys talk about using trout roe as an excellent bait. When Peggy wasn't looking, I used my Zen and changed my worm into trout roe. It didn't take long until I reeled in a twenty-eight-inch rainbow trout. I made more roe and chummed the water with it -another trick I learned from the boy. I couldn't keep up with the fish. I kept pulling them in. Peggy caught two, but I could tell that my success bothered her.

"Are you sure you are using the same worms as me?"

I shrugged and tried to stop the smile that wanted to appear. I ended up catching sixteen fish.

Thursday at dinner, Peggy made a giant pot of fish soup.

"This is the best," Christian said.

"Let's have more dinners like this," Mike said as he looked into the empty pot.

I only got half of a cup of soup. I watched as the greedy Sanibels snorted down my soup so fast they didn't even have time to taste it. I say my soup because it was my fish they were consuming. I regretted not keeping the fish for myself. They didn't pause for breaths. Sloppy broth rolled down chins. They grunted and pushed as they defended their food from each other, reminding me of a pen of filthy pigs. They disgusted me. My belly groaned, and I used my Zen to expand the drops of soup left in my bowl, giving me as much soup as I wanted.

THE DAY FINALLY ARRIVED. Our camping trip! Besides the cot in the storage shed, the Sanibels didn't have a lick of camping equipment. Thankfully, they knew the whole town and scrounged up enough gear for all fourteen of us. Even Mike came, leaving his precious XBOX behind, alone in the house with no one to molest it for the night.

The campground host made us get three campsites. Two were together, and the third was four spots over. I ended up being in the third site. I shared it with Alashia, Emma, and Hillary. When the tents were all set up, Peggy had us help her make Dutch oven chicken and rolls.

"I have never cooked in one of these before," she said. "My ancestors did, though."

I don't think she fired the briquettes long enough because they barely stayed warm after she spread them on the ovens.

"I don't get what I am doing wrong. It has been over three hours, and the chicken is still pink," Peggy growled, kicking at the dust next to the fire pit.

"Let's just go home. This whole idea is way too much work," Mike said.

"You just want to go home to play your stupid video game. It is good for us to get a break from technology," Peggy yelled.

The two ended up in a huge argument, with many kids taking one side or the other. I left the intense fighting and sat alone in my camping spot. I picked up a rock, turned it into a knife, and then carved a stick. As little slivers of bark flew off, inspiration hit me.

I returned to the central camp spot and used my Zen to cook everything in the three Dutch ovens.

"I think it's done," I said.

"There is no way it is done," Mike barked. "Your idiot mother didn't heat the briquettes long enough. Now, we are all going to starve while there is a house full of food only a few miles away.

"I really think it's done," I tried again.

"We could run to Burger King," Hillary said, looking for an escape to civilization.

"Can I check it?" I asked.

"You're wasting your time," Mike said. "Burger King does sound good."

"I don't mind," I said, lifting the lid. Steam spilled out as the lid seared into my hand, instantly burning it. I dropped the sizzling top into the dirt and ran to the stream to cool my hand.

While I had my hand in the stream, the family huddled around the ovens like ravenous vultures. Not one person cared about my accident. I knew they would devour every drop of food before I returned. The heavenly aroma made me extra hungry. I wasn't going to miss out. I had a plan. I had to stop them.

Whenever someone reached into an oven, I sent an electric shock to them.

"Ouch," Peggy screamed as she dropped the serving spoon in the dirt.

"What did you do that for?" Mike growled. "Now we can't use the spoon."

"Ouch!"

"Ooohh!"

"Owie!!" others screeched as they were zapped. They kept trying for the food, but all stopped when they were shocked. After several shocks, the family backed away from the food, eying it like it was demonic.

When my hand cooled, I grabbed a plate and walked to the table. And for the first time among the Sanibels, they parted to let me at the food. All watched, waiting to see me electrocuted. I reached in with my spoon and took three huge, towering scoopfuls, plopping them on my plate. I then sat down in a camping chair as everyone watched in silent amazement, wondering how I hadn't been shocked.

Traydon decided to brave it again. He ever so carefully reached into the dish and grabbed the spoon. Nothing happened. He carefully scooped out a generous helping of food. Nothing. Since he had no competition, he, too, took three huge spoonfuls and sat by me. He smiled at me as if we were in a class of our own, a class untouchable. Within seconds, when the rest of the family found the danger of electrocution was gone, they pushed and fought to fill their plates.

Later, Mike tried to build a fire for us to gather around. He had no scout skills. Every time he got a small flame under the wood, it went out. I knew nothing about constructing fires, but there had to be a better way. I couldn't take any more of his failure and ignited the wood in the firepit. Giant flames danced on the wood, and Mike, proud of his fire starting-skills, danced around the fire.

"I am Lord of the Fire," he sang, doing a silly dance. His enthusiasm flamed through the family, and soon, all fourteen of us wildly danced around the fire. We sang, chanted, and let go of our inhibitions.

That night will always be one of my favorite memories.

After our dancing died, Corbon and Hillary brought out guitars, and we sang songs around the campfire. I noticed the aura connecting us was violet, flowing in a wave around and above us, uniting us all together. The energy field was strong as it radiated in and out of us. I never wanted to leave.

<hr>

"TIME TO GET UP AND get ready for church," Peggy said, shaking me in my cot.

Sleepily, I peered at her. I wasn't ready to wake up yet. "Hey, doesn't your religion believe in free agency?" I asked.

"Of course, we do," she said in her cartoon voice. She peered over me, and I could taste her strong BO. Didn't she want to shower and show her church what a perfect woman she was? I tried to pull the blankets over my head, but she grabbed them and stopped me.

"Well, then, don't I have the agency to skip church?" I couldn't stand having her face right above mine.

"Sure you do, but free agency doesn't mean you can skip out on consequences.'

"What do you mean?"

"Well, let's say you want to steal a candy bar from the store. You have the free agency to do it. But, when they haul you to jail, you don't have the agency to escape the punishment. Does that make sense?"

"So, what is the punishment if I don't go to church?" I asked.

"Oh, I wouldn't think of punishing anyone for not going to church." She brought her head even closer to mine.

"So, you don't mind if I don't go?"

"I don't mind at all, for you have free agency," Peggy said. She thinned her lips into a sly smile.

"Good," I said, rolling onto my stomach. "Cause I think I am going to stay home today."

"That is fine, but don't bother coming to family dinner tonight. Those who skip church miss dinner." As she walked away, she said, "Oh yeah, and those who don't go to church, don't get to go out on the boat."

Although I wanted to rebel, for some reason, I couldn't. When the family left for church, I was with them.

While we were gone for church, a bowling ball had rolled down the stairs and landed on the TV. Fragments of glass and broken TV must have showered over the family room because shards of glass were everywhere. Peggy spent the evening in her room sulking and didn't take me out on the reservoir.

She hadn't kept her deal. One of the reasons I went to church was so she could take me out. I decided to forgive her since we had learned about service and forgiveness at church.

The next night, the family decided to go to Brigham City and get a *Busy Bee Snowcone*. I heard they were tasty but wasn't in the mood to go. I needed a break from the loud, obnoxious family. Besides, I could make my own snowcone while they were gone.

Alone, I rested on the couch. As I relaxed, my hand throbbed where I had burnt it with the Dutch oven on Saturday. I noticed it was inflamed with a big blister on it.

Why hadn't I healed myself before now? Sometimes, I forget I could do so much. I watched as the skin renewed itself. My flesh returned to a soft pink.

"I am all-powerful!" I jumped up and danced around the table. "I healed myself!" If I could heal others, imagine the good I could do for the world. I could become a doctor and heal whoever came into my clinic. I would charge a minimal fee, thus allowing my services to everyone. I ran into the bathroom, got my foot caught in garbage, and tripped into a pile of mildewy rags. The black growth from the rags had moved into the rug. It made me sick, but it gave me an idea.

They had talked about service in church, and I wanted to do some type of service. Now I had my chance. What better service could I offer than to clean the Sanibel's pigsty home? I remembered I had vowed never to clean it again, but this time, I would do it for God.

This time was much easier because I used the surrounding energy to finish it all quickly.

"I am the best," I said, eating my snow cone. When I had cleaned, I had also fixed the TV. I took a bite of the tiger's blood snow cone, and a rush of pain moved into my head. I used my Zen to stop it and then looked at the TV. "Why did I fix that?" I sent it to the outside trash and threw it away. Peggy and Mike would be better off without it.

I sat again on the couch. No one had used the family room since the TV had broken and filled the area with sharp glass. Something pinched my butt.

"Did I miss some glass?" I looked under me and realized the couch spring was pinching me. "I can fix that," I said as the couch became new under the stained cushions. Why stop there? I made the upholstery new, then made all the carpet new as well.

I was out in the shed when the van pulled up. I stayed to the side of the house until the family had gone inside. Falling in line, I walked in with everyone. I didn't want them to know it had been me who had cleaned the house. They'd probably think I was with them the whole time.

"What happened in here?" Peggy exclaimed.

"Everything is new!" Hillary said.

"Oh my heck, the walls are fixed," Mike shouted. "I could kiss whoever fixed the walls. I had been meaning to do that."

"Mercy, mercy, mercy me!"

Everyone walked from room to room in utter shock. All the auras were light green. I loved their reaction as they tried to decide how their house had gotten so clean and repaired.

"Church members, for sure."

"I think it was the Whipples."

"It was a miracle."

Before we went to bed, I said. "Hey, I have a suggestion. This is the best I have ever seen your house."

"This is the best I have ever seen my house," Peggy said.

"Why don't we *All* try to keep it that way? Other families do. Why don't we? For instance, put garbage in the trash cans instead of the floor. Why don't we wash our own dishes after we use them? Why don't we do what we can to keep this place nice?"

Everyone happily agreed, probably affected by the calming energy coming from the clean house.

THE NEXT DAY WAS A long, boring summer day with nothing exciting happening. I lazed around the house, seriously under-stimulated. I had spent the time at Harvard with every second of my time accounted for. Now, I had nothing going on. I wasn't complaining. It was a nice break, but it still made me restless. Peggy didn't take us out on the boat that night. I think she was still loathing having her TV gone.

Wednesday, I woke up bright and early. I had a plan. I wanted to go exploring. I had lots of maps in my head of the mountain terrain. Despite my bad experience before, I hitched hiked with a nice old lady. It took some doing, but I got the driver to drop me off in the middle of Logan Canyon.

"I don't feel good about leaving a kid alone in the canyon. What if something bad happens to you? I would never forgive myself," she said when I had her pull over on a shoulder next to a trail.

"Remember, I told you my uncle has a cabin up the mountain from here."

The old lady looked at the high peak. "It looks too rocky for a cabin."

I pointed to a small dirt trail. "Oh, but he does. He's been sick, and I am going to take care of him," I lied.

"How does he get things to his cabin on that small trail? Like furniture, for instance?"

"Oh, there is a small service road that comes from the other side of the mountain that leads to the cabin, but it is really far from here. I use the trail because it is much faster and closer."

She looked like she accepted the idea a little more, but then she said, "I don't feel good about this."

"I'll be fine," I said as I climbed out. "And I promise you, my uncle will thank you for this." I hurried and closed the door before she could protest anymore. I quickly bounded up the small dirt trail. She sat in her car, watching me until I was out of sight.

I had gone there because I wanted to explore my abilities more. I knew I would find a nice, safe place up in the mountains. I needed to be alone. I had studied the topography maps in my head and knew where a cave was.

The side of the mountain had been way steeper than I had anticipated. To my knowledge, I had never climbed a mountain before.

"This is harder than I thought it would be," I growled through shortened breaths. The steeper things got, the harder it became. My feet slipped often, and I kept scrapping open my hands. I would heal them with my Zen, turn around, and do it again. I soon came to an edge where I had to reach high and over to grab a protruding rock. I held on to it and proceeded to pull my body up. Only halfway over the rock's lip, I found myself stuck. I was in such a position I could not go up, and I couldn't go down. As I held on for my life, my arms tired, burning as I tried to keep myself in place. They ached and screamed at me, and my fingers started to slip. I tried to reposition my hands, but that was foolish. I lost my hold, and I fell. My hip banged into a boulder. Then I went straight down with no rocks to stop me or to crash into. I could tell I was about a hundred feet above the next ledge of rocks as my body somersaulted down the mountain. As I rushed downward, dread filled me.

Suddenly, I remembered making Nathan fly. Centimeters before I crashed into the ground, I grabbed the energy field around me and lifted my body. A couple of bushes from the ground scratched me as I rose above them.

My Zen had saved me.

I couldn't believe it! I hadn't crashed. I had saved my life, and I had learned to fly!

Flying wasn't like I had imagined. I had always thought that if one could fly, they would will themselves to do it. But that wasn't how it worked. I was flying by the collection and movement of energy around me. It took constant vigilance to make sure the energy was always there. When I got excited and distracted, the momentum would disappear, and I would begin to plummet down.

Besides the work it took to keep me in the air, it was the most fantastic experience: flying above the ground, feeling the wind rush through my hair, and defy the laws of gravity.

I spent the next few hours mastering and perfecting the gift of flight. When I felt confident in my skills, I decided to go to the cave like I had initially planned to. Good thing I had learned to fly because there was no way I could not have made it to the cave otherwise. The mountain was too rugged and steep for my skills. I flew myself to the cave and went in.

Instantly, the darkness enveloped me. I gathered the bands of light from outside and brought them in, illuminating the cavern.

"The cave isn't as big as I hoped." I sighed.

I had read a story back at ACYI about a girl who took a great adventure in a cave. She had explored many caverns, each one more glorious than the next, but in my cave, there were only three rooms. I had dreamed of discovering crystals and gems. But none of that was in the cave.

For the longest time, I had wanted my own space, a place I could call my own. In a way, I already had it out in the shed, but I desired a place where I could experiment, and in the shed, I couldn't do that.

Between the plants, the soil, the rocks, and the air, I had all the elements on the mountain to do whatever I wanted.

I dissolved bonds, recreated bonds, and restructured molecular elements with my Zen.

"I am the master of atoms. Robert Oppenheimer would be jealous."

I decided to make myself a bedroom in the first room. I took some of the rock from the cave wall and brought it out and up, creating a rock-bed.

"This is dope."

I looked at the cold, hard bed. It would need a blanket. I ripped a small strip off my shirt and created a large, fluffy blanket.

In the next cavern, I formed rocks into two couches.

I sat and shifted around on the hard couches. They weren't soft, but their marbled design made them awesome!

In the last room, I created a dining table out of rock.

If someone had watched me, they would have thought I had magic. I had seen several movies about witches who could do anything with magic. I knew all those shows were fantasy, but if they weren't, maybe magic meant the power to control the atoms and molecules and create them into things. If one could believe in magic, one could unquestionably believe in my abilities to form molecules into whatever I desired. I did not use some unknown, mystical force, but I used math and science. For me, the ability to do this seemed simple, as if everyone should be able to figure it out.

"My castle is complete," I said, sitting on the couch. I pretended to be a princess, imagining the cave larger than it was, filled with servants and animals. I hadn't done much pretending in life, and I liked being a kid.

The evening approached; I realized how far I was from home. I probably needed to start making my way there. I hated to leave my cave. Not only I had designed it, but I had allowed myself to enter a world of fantasy. I allowed myself to be a kid. Rapture filled my soul. With all the knowledge stored in me, I probably hadn't played as a kid. It felt good to know I was doing what normal kids did.

I went to an open space outside the cave and noticed birds in the trees. Their beautiful song made me smile.

"Can I make something living?"

I gathered the elements together and formed them into a small bird. I shook as I held it. It was beautiful without blemish, every feather perfect. I turned it repeatedly in my hand, but there was no life to it. It was more like a toy than something living. I might be able to manipulate elements, but did I know how to create life?

Chapter 12

I FLEW DOWN TO THE side of the road. As a group of cars approached, I put my thumb out, and a car pulled over in twenty minutes. It was a lone man. His aura was mustard yellow. Something inside me screamed, *run!*

Without waiting to hear what he had to say, I turned and ran. There wasn't anywhere for me to go. The rocks went straight up the mountain, but I tried to climb up them.

"Hey, get back here," he screamed.

His car door screeched open. I looked behind me, hoping to see cars approaching, but we were alone. I tried again to climb up the mountain, but at this spot, it seemed impossible. Twigs and branches snapped as he was almost right behind me. My head felt light, and I needed to pee. I could hear him breathe, and my hair stood up as I shook. I had no choice.

I flew over his head as he madly tried to grab my leg.

I had learned my lesson. I would never hitchhike again! I decided to fly the rest of the way home. Since it was dark, I doubted that anyone would see me. It got cold quickly, and I formed my shirt into a jacket, but it didn't help much. I gathered the surrounding energy and made ATP; instantly, every part of me was warm.

When I got home, I went straight to the shed.

THE FOLLOWING DAY, Peggy was excitedly waking me up.

"KRL news is here!" she said. "And they want to do a story on you!"

I rubbed the sleep out of my eyes. "Why do they want to do a story on me?" I asked. I could feel my muscles ache from the hiking I had done.

"Because they found out about your doctorate you are getting at Harvard."

"Did you tell them?" I asked.

"No, I promise I didn't."

I guessed they must have heard about it from someone at church. Peggy had bragged to everyone about my Harvard opportunity. I don't think she was proud of me. I think she liked the bragging rights of being my foster mom. She would tell everyone how I could neither talk nor read. But, after staying with the Sanibels, I had become a genius.

Out of the suitcase, I picked out a small business suit, one of my best outfits. It made me look sophisticated and hip.

"What should I do with my hair?" I had no idea.

I peeked out the door and found two film crew members bustling about. I didn't want to look stupid as I entered the house with undone hair. I took the fibers in my hair and made them straight and smooth. I looked at my spindly arms. I always thought I looked like a starving skeleton. Living with the Sanibels hadn't added any meat to my frame. I decided to bring a little definition to my body. I hypertrophied my muscles, making them bigger, and added a little fat to my hips. I caused the door to become reflective as I looked at myself. Still not satisfied, I infused dark highlights in my golden white hair.

"Yes," I said quietly. I could dig this new look.

With my improved appearance, I entered the house through the side door. It was messy but still relatively clean from Monday, -way better than it usually looked. Thankfully, I had fixed up their house. I wouldn't have met the TV crew if their house had been trashed like before.

When I walked into the family room, the news anchor stood up with her hands stretched out, taking my hand and vigorously shaking it up and down. The sweat from her hands slimed me, and I wanted mine back.

"Hi, I am Karen Pieffer from KRL news. We heard about your admission to Harvard and wanted to do a news story on you. Is that all right, Alora?" She said, still shaking my hand up and down.

She called me Alora! "Sure," I said.

"Is that still all right with you, Mrs. Sanibel? We talked to your husband on the phone and set everything up last night." I looked over at Peggy. She was staring at me. She could tell I looked different, but she couldn't place it. "Is Mike Sanibel here?"

"He's at work, and he didn't mention this to me."

"Is that all right with you?" Karen asked again. "We already got written permission from Child Protective Services. We need yours," she said.

Peggy snapped out of her trance. "What do I get out of it?" she asked.

"What do you mean?" Karen asked, squinting her brow.

"What do I get if I let Alora on your news show?"

"Well, you get to share with Utah what a wonderful daughter you have."

"But you are not going to pay me anything for it?" Leave it to Peggy to make this all about her.

In the kitchen, Christian and Elizabeth were fighting about something. The news crew looked toward the kitchen.

"Shut it," Peggy screamed, but they didn't respond. No one ever listened to her. The TV crew tensed. I had to do something. I sent my Zen into the kitchen and numbed their vocal cords.

Karen turned back to Peggy. "Well?" Peggy asked.

"That's not how we do it. We don't generally pay to put someone on the news. Most people are eager to be on it for free."

"I see, so you make a profit off my daughter, and we make nothing."

"Stop it, Mom," Hillary said in embarrassment.

"Stay out of this, Hillary," Peggy said. She turned back to Karen. "I know you can't put Alora on without my consent. I will only give it if you give me something for it."

Karen's producer stepped forward, holding two fifty-dollar gift cards to Olive Garden. "How about some nice gift certificates for dinner," he said.

Peggy thought about it for a moment. "Fine, but I want to be on your news with her."

"Great," they both responded, happy to have gotten her permission.

I was given a quick briefing while the film crew rearranged the room, and Peggy signed the paperwork.

"I really like it outside. Can we do it with the reservoir behind me?" I asked.

"Yes, that sounds like a great shot," the producer said. "Everyone, outside."

The cool air seemed to make everyone relax, even Peggy. We followed the camera crew around until they found their perfect shot. They pulled chairs out of their van and had a set put together within seconds, sitting us directly in front of the reservoir.

"Remember, this is live," Karin reminded us. "Don't be scared, Alora, you will do great."

The cameraman counted down, and we were on live TV before I could breathe. It was then I remembered I hadn't used the bathroom yet.

"This is Karen Pieffer with KRL News. I am here today with Alora Funk, who has quite a story. Alora is thirteen years old, and if you remember, we brought you the exclusive story of how she had been found captive in a cement room earlier in March. We have been watching her story to keep you, the viewers, informed. I believe you will all be relieved to llearn Alora has found a loving home with a beautiful family, and she has been well cared for. But what makes this story remarkable is Alora is not like most thirteen-year-old girls. She is exceptionally brilliant, and while other girls her age spent their summer waterskiing and chasing boys, Alora was at an exclusive summer camp at Harvard University.

"We have a conference call right now with Dr. Van Hassel, the director of the science program at Harvard. Hello, Dr. Van Hassel." I couldn't see him but could hear him in my earpiece.

"Hello, Ms. Karen Pieffer."

"Doctor, how did you find out about Alora's exceptional gifts in the sciences?"

"A well-trusted source had given me a tip." By that, he meant Marge.

"I heard you personally flew to Mantua to meet this starlet and invite her back to your elite summer camp."

"Indeed, I did."

"Is it true you get over a thousand applicants a year for this camp, and you only accept twenty?"

"That is true."

"And is it true Alora hadn't even applied to this camp? That you flew all the way out here and begged her to follow you back?" Karen looked so natural in what she did. How was she not scared with the camera constantly on her? Her aura was blue-violet, one of confidence. Peggy's was light pink; I don't remember seeing hers that color before. Her huge smile filled her face. She loved playing the part of the mother of a genius. My aura was ice blue since I was so scared. I had to pee so bad I could hardly think about anything else.

"Now Karen, don't put words into my mouth. I did not beg, nor would I ever beg. I opened the opportunity for this child, and she accepted it," I heard Dr. Van Hassel say in my earpiece.

"I heard she had a private sponsor who paid for her airfare, her admission to the program, her wardrobe, and other expenses in the amount of eighteen thousand, two hundred and twenty-two dollars."

"Karen, I don't believe you dragged me to this phone interview to discuss the expenses, did you?" Dr. Van Hassel's voice went stiff and tight.

"Let's talk about Alora's performance at the school," Karen responded.

"Stalwart!"

"Were you disappointed by your decision to make a spot for her?"

"I never regretted it. She was the best student we have ever had in our program." I could hear the pride in Dr. Van Hassel's voice. I beamed at his compliments.

"And is it true your university is willing to give her a doctorate right now?"

"We will not *GIVE* her a doctorate! She will earn it."

"What are your plans for her?"

"She is brilliant, and we intend to assist her in adding knowledge to her skill set. After she graduates, we are prepared to offer her a position on our faculty to help aid us in our research and development programs. Ms. Alora Funk has a promising future, and we want to hold her hand every step of the way."

"Thank you, Dr. Van Hassel."

"And thank you, Karen Pieffer."

"Let us turn to Alora. This must all come as a big shock to you. You didn't know who you were back in March. You didn't even know how to speak. What changed? How did you find this intellectually brilliant side of yourself?"

What do I say? I didn't know how to answer her. I wanted to crawl back into my cocoon. Karen looked uncomfortable by my lack of response, so I shrugged. Peggy didn't miss a minute to fluff her feathers.

"She found her intellect because our family took her in, and we used every opportunity we had to tutor her and educate her."

A loud truck roared behind us. The TV crew didn't respond, but Peggy and I turned and looked at it.

"So, you are saying because of your influence, Alora has become a child protégée?"

We both turned back to Karen.

I tried to keep from wiggling in my chair because I had to go to the bathroom so badly. My bladder threatened to pop right there on live TV.

"Darn straight," Peggy gloated.

Karen turned back to me. "Will you keep us informed on your journey at Harvard? Can we come and visit you out there?"

"Sure," I said, feeling my face flush.

"Thank you, Sanibels, thank you Alora. This is Karen Pieffer from KRL News doing an exclusive interview with Alora Funk. I turn the time back to you, Grant."

———◈———

THE NEWS CREW WAS GONE within minutes, and I felt so weird. I couldn't imagine all the people sitting around in their homes watching me on TV. It didn't seem natural.

As we walked back into the house, Peggy turned to me. "You look different today," she observed.

"Hmm, I am not sure why," I responded.

"Well, whatever you did, it looks good."

I ran to the bathroom. When I was done, I looked at myself in the mirror. I liked the fuller face. I had always seemed so thin and sickly. Even my darker highlights made me look better. Before, my hair had been so blond I always thought it looked white, like an old lady.

———◈———

AS I WALKED TO THE highway, a burst of negative energy consumed me. My hair stood on end, and I knew something was wrong. I looked around until I saw a stray dog rushing toward me. The huge Rottweiler came straight at me. I didn't have time to think as I ran. Foolishly, I tried to push it away, but its teeth sunk into my hand, and the pain exploded in me.

What do I do? I could hardly breathe, let alone think, as I tried to free my arm from its teeth. Hot saliva soaked my skin. I had to do something.

Wait. I have my Zen.

The dog rocketed through the sky. Out of pure fear, I hit it with a deadly force. Its body limply crashed to the ground; all signs of life gone.

"What have I done!" I screamed. Cautiously, I went to the prone dog on the ground. I picked up a stick and poked it into its side. Nothing happened. Its aura had changed from mustard yellow to grey. I poked a little harder. Still no reaction. I looked at its chest to see if it was breathing. There was no movement.

I killed a dog.

I dropped to the dog's side and wrapped my body over it and bawled deep, heavy cries.

"I was only trying to protect myself. I never meant to kill you."

My soul ached.

"Please come back to life, please," I begged. I shook the dog. Horror and dread filled me.

As I cried, I had an idea. If I killed the dog with my Zen, then maybe I could bring it back to life with my Zen. With that thought, I filled the dog with positive energy, hoping to bring it back to life. Nothing. I gathered the most energy I ever had and shot it into the dog. Its body flew two feet, but still no signs of life.

I draped my body again over the Rottweiler and howled in sorrow. I had never meant to kill it. As I cried, I could hear a car coming around the corner. I quickly stood up and hid behind a hedge. I didn't want to get in trouble for killing a dog. To my terror, the car noticed the dead dog and stopped. I crawled along the hedge, trying not to be seen until I was around the corner and out of sight.

Then I ran.

I was so disturbed. I had to get to the cave and figure things out. Even though I knew how to fly, I didn't dare do it in the daylight. So, again, I took my chances on hitchhiking, being more careful about who I held my thumb out to.

I found a ride with a young girl on her way to USU. There, I eventually found another ride through Logan Canyon with a group of college students. They didn't care about dropping off a young girl in the middle of a canyon. Once they pulled away, I hiked up through the thick mountainside until I knew I was out of sight from the road. Then I picked up the energy around me and flew to my castle cave.

When I got there, I landed, and instead of going inside, I sat outside the cave in meditation. I decided to create fire, and it hovered above my hand for a moment. I experimented with making it get bigger and then smaller. I even tried to make it burn without the intense heat. As I practiced with fire, I thought of the time in the study group when everyone chose what superpower they wanted. Nate said he wanted to fly. Steve said he wanted to control fire. What would they think if they both could see me now? I could fly and control fire!

My hand throbbed, and my thoughts returned to the dog I had murdered. The remembrance made me sick. My hand had swollen from the dog bite. I thought about healing it but decided I didn't deserve to heal my hand. I had killed a dog. The bite was my punishment. I didn't want to get sick from bacteria, so I used my Zen to clean out the cut, but I left it to heal naturally.

Chapter 13

SCHOOL WAS ABOUT TO start, and Peggy took us shopping in Brigham City to pick out school supplies. I could hardly focus on what I needed because a tense vibration jiggled my brain. It had started the night before, and there was nothing I could do to stop it as it rattled through my bones. I tried to ignore it while I was looking at folders with Hillary. As I did, I could hear a conversation on the other side of the aisle. It was between a man and a woman. Their voices were *very familiar*. As I listened, I suddenly realized they spoke in Russian the whole time, and I understood everything they were saying.

And then it hit me.

I knew those voices!

Since my liberation, I hadn't had too many sure moments in my life, but I was convinced beyond a shadow of a doubt the voices I heard belonged to Vyacheslav and Nadezhda, my Russian captures.

I felt like I was trapped in a silent movie where everything moved fast, except me. Hadn't Mr. Cox or someone told me that the Russians had been sent to jail? What were they doing here? In Brigham? I was tempted to peek around the aisle and look at them, but I didn't want them to see me. They would recognize me before I would recognize them. In a panic, I ran from the aisle, leaving Hillary behind.

"Where are you going, Alora?" she called loudly behind me.

"Shhh," I said as I left the aisle. I madly searched the store for Peggy. I seemed to run into a Sanibel in every aisle since there were thirteen of us there, but for the life of me, it felt like I would never find Peggy. Finally, after a desperate search, I found her in the cheese section.

"We need to go!" I said, out of breath.

"Mercy me, Alora, slow down. What is going on?" She brought a pack of cheese to her nose and smelled it.

"They are here," I said through deep breaths.

"Who is here?" she said, half listening to me. She peeled a piece of the plastic away and took a tiny nibble of the cheese. Her face squinted. "That one doesn't taste good," she said, returning it to the case.

"The Russians," I said back.

"That's nice," she said, grabbing a package of blueberry goat cheese.

"You don't understand. These are the people who kept me in the cement room."

I had her attention. She dropped the cheese on the floor and looked at me, her eyes filling with concern.

"Alora, the Russians who hurt you were put in jail."

"Maybe they were, but I guarantee they are here in this store right now."

"Did you see them?" she asked. She looked frightened.

"No."

"Then how do you know they are here?"

"Because I heard them."

Peggy's face relaxed. "Honey, you probably heard someone speaking Russian and assumed it was them."

"No," I said firmly. "I heard them, and I know it was them. There is no mistake. It was them."

Peggy looked worried again. "What should we do, Alora?" She gazed around the dairy section.

"We need to get out of here," I replied.

Peggy looked at her overflowing cart. "I can't leave all these things. There is no way I am coming back tonight or Monday. No way! This shopping trip has already stolen an hour of my time."

"Well, I must go," I said, walking backward, tripping over my feet. The Russians could be anywhere in the store. It didn't help I had no idea what they looked like.

Peggy opened her mammoth purse and sorted through all her belongings. She seemed to take forever. I was ready to run all the way back to Mantua if she didn't hurry. "Now, where are those keys," she said.

"Will you hurry?"

"Yes, yes, of course," she said as she continued to look for her keys. She didn't act at all like my life was at stake. I couldn't wait for her. Without saying anything, I ran.

"Hey Alora!" she called after me. Could she have said it any louder?

I carefully made my way through the store, trying to avoid any couple who were together. Once outside, I ran to the van. I looked around the parking lot to ensure no couple was in sight. There were only families and teens. I looked at the van, sent my Zen into it, and undid the lock. Again, I looked around and then ducked inside the vehicle. I locked the door and lay on the bottom of the van.

Peggy wasn't true to her word because she was in the store for another hour. Didn't she care about my safety? A few kids returned to the van.

"Alora, let us in," they screamed. What were they doing? If the Russian couple were around, then they would hear them. I quickly sat up and unlocked the doors. Over time, the family poured in with all their loudness. Peggy was left alone to load all the groceries and school supplies into the back of the van. I would have hopped out to help her, but I didn't want to be seen, so I stayed low while the bags of merchandise piled around me. Soon, everyone was in, and we drove back home.

I didn't stay in the shed that night but on the floor of my old bedroom. I had a hard time sleeping.

What if the Russians followed us home?

Also, the vibration in my head made it hard to sleep.

The next day at church, I was taken aback by the celebrity status I had gained. Everyone came up and congratulated me on being on the news. It was so weird.

I tried to dismiss my fear about the Russians as I decided to sleep in the shed. The vibration in my head made it hard to sleep, but eventually I did.

Bark. Bark. The mad barking of Athena woke me as she clawed on the door. It was past midnight, and my mind was in a daze, so I opened the shed door, and Athena barreled out. She ran to the house door and clawed and barked at it.

Maybe there is a fire in the house. I had heard a story at school about how a dog had saved a family from a fire. I ran to the door to let Athena in. As I reached the door, I noticed a car parked at the side of the house. My heart stopped beating.

Was there someone in the house?

Suddenly, clarity hit me as I thought about the Russians from the store.

I slowly crawled below the windows and peeked inside. I could see the family gathered in the family room with the couple's back to me.

The Russians!

The Russians were in my home!

I almost became paralyzed by fear. I had no idea what to do. My logical mind seemed to shut down on me.

What should I do? I could hear Athena tearing at the door, still wanting to be let in. I went to the side door and, with shaking hands, let Athena in. I did not follow. If nothing else, maybe she would attack the intruders. My legs gave out, and I dropped to the ground. Part of me wanted to run and disappear. The other part wanted to go inside and save my family. I knew going in to save them was foolish.

I ducked into a bush. That's when I heard a gunshot go off. The silence that followed was heavy. My heart tried to rip out of my chest. My head spun.

Who had they shot? Why would they shoot anyone? I no longer felt safe in the bush. I had to get out of there. I looked around for a better hiding spot. At first, I thought about taking cover in the van, but surely, they would look there. I almost decided to take off in the van, but then I thought against it. What if the Sanibels needed to escape? Finally, I decided to take the Russians' car.

I ran over to it and found it locked. I reached my Zen in and unlocked the doors. Once inside, I sat in the driver's seat and, with my Zen, turned the car on. I put the gear shift into drive like I had seen Peggy do. The car shot forward, and I found I had no control over it. Peggy had made driving look so easy, but it raced down the road, and I couldn't steady or stop it. The tires skidded as I tried to use the brakes, but I couldn't really touch the brakes since the seat was so far back. The car jerked up the street until it crashed into a tree.

With smoke everywhere, I jumped out of the car, leaving it behind. I ran down the street until I got to the campground. I tried to hide beside someone's tent, but the dog inside started barking at me. In fear, I ran out of the campground.

I crouched on the ground and rocked back and forth. "What do I do?" I sobbed as my body shook.

I could fly to my castle-cave, but it was such a long way.

I didn't want the Russians to get me and put me in a medical coma again. What if they put me in one, and I lost all of the knowledge I had been gaining and never got it back? I didn't want to lose my memories of the Sanibels and Mantua. I couldn't let them catch me.

I finally decided to fly to Marge's house. When I got there, I was too scared to wake her. I crawled onto her trampoline and waited the rest of the night out on it.

I must have fallen asleep after the sun had risen because I woke up to Marge standing over me. The first sensation I noticed was the intense vibration still in my head.

"Alora, what are you doing on my tramp? Does Peggy know you are here?"

"The Russians came to my house last night," I shrieked. "They broke into it and shot someone. I don't know who, but I heard the gunshot." I could hardly control my speech as my voice fluttered up and down.

"What are you talking about?" Marge asked. She stood in her pajamas as the sun rose behind her. I shivered to the cold, damp dew that soaked my clothes. I used ATP to dry and warm me.

"The Russians, the ones who had kept me in the cement room. They found me and broke into our house last night." I pulled my legs under me and wrapped my arms around them. Cars drove next to the house. It surprised me how much more traffic there was in Brigham City compared to Mantua.

"I thought they were in jail," Margre sounded just like Peggy.

"Obviously, they are not," I shouted.

"Have you called the police?" Margre asked. Her hands flew over her mouth as her eyes looked worried. Her aura was teal, while mine was ice-blue.

"No, I didn't know what to do, so I came here."

"Why didn't you wake me?" Margre asked. "How long have you been here?" She waved her hands at me, inviting me to get closer. I scooted a little toward her, but not fully.

"Because I was afraid it was too late to knock on your door."

"That is foolish. You are welcome to knock on my door any hour of the night, especially if there is an emergency."

Margre hugged me, and I followed her inside. She picked up her phone and called 911.

"Yes, I have Alora Funk here with me...Yes, the one who was on the news...yes, that is her. She said her home was broken into last night, and the Russians who had been keeping her in a cement room had broken in and hurt her family...No, I don't think so. Let me ask her. Alora, are you hurt?" I shook my head no. "No, she isn't. But you need to send someone over to her house right away."

MARGRE CALLED CHILD Protective Services, and they came and picked me up and drove me to their office, where I was left in a room for most of the day. They brought in toys and teddy bears to appease me, and some lady sat with me the whole time, asking me a ton of questions. I was so tired. At some point, I fell asleep. When I woke up, my neck was stiff. The only nice thing was the vibration in my head had stopped.

Finally, Mr. Cox came into the room.

"Well, Alora, that was pretty scary. We figured the Russians found you by your news program. I don't know who authorized you to be on the news. I will have to look into that. No one had told us the Russians had escaped jail last week. That would have been good to know."

"Oh, how stupid of me," I said. Why had I gone on the news?

"We need to get you someplace safe. We can put you in the crisis nursery for a week or two while we find a good placement for you. We are thinking about sending you out of state."

Crisis Nursery! That was the last place I wanted to go. It had been a great place for me initially, but I felt I was too old to return there. Besides, I was going to Harvard. "I will be going to Harvard next week. That is out of state."

"We can longer send you there because the Russians will know exactly where to find you. You won't be closely watched at Harvard, and it wouldn't be hard for them to apprehend you."

I had a hard time comprehending what he said. Who were these Russians? Why weren't they in jail? Why did they want me? Who were they working for? Why must my life be stopped because of them? It was all too overwhelming. "What are you saying? I can't go to Harvard?" I desperately asked.

"At least not until the Russians are back behind bars."

"Did the police not catch them after we called 911?"

"No, the Russians were long gone by the time they got there."

"Did they kill my family?" It was a tricky question to ask. I feared what his answer would be.

"No."

"Well, who did they shoot?"

"They shot the dog."

"Athena!" I screamed as my hands went across my mouth. I should have never sent her into the house. It was my fault.

"Don't worry. They said it only hit her left hind leg. The dog didn't die."

A little peace entered me, knowing Athena would be all right and that none of my family had been shot.

"I really want to go to Harvard because they are going to let me earn a doctorate," I said. I didn't think it was fair that the Russians could stop me from going.

"If they were going to give it to you once, they will give it to you again."

I put my head in my hands and sobbed. Every locked-up emotion poured out of me. Dread and darkness filled my soul and turned my aura gray.

When I had slowed down, I turned to Mr. Cox. "I don't want to go back to the crisis nursery. I want to go home to the Sanibels."

"It is no longer safe for you or them to have you there."

I put my hands over my face and kept crying. After a few minutes, I sat up again. "Can I go to the Petersons?"

"Alora, it would be best to place you out of state at this time."

"Okay, I understand, but can I go there at least until you find me an out-of-state home? I don't want to go back to the crisis nursery."

After going to Harvard, I felt more grown up. The crisis nursery made me feel like a baby.

"I will see," Mr. Cox said as he left me.

When he returned, he had a faint smile on his face. "It looks like you can stay with the Petersons until we can place you out of state. But you must stay low. You can't go to the store, you can't go to the park, and you can't go to church. Since you have been on the news several times, people will know your face. You must stay low."

"Okay."

⸺ ◉ ⸺

MY LIFE FELT OUT OF control. I lay in the Petersons' bedroom and bawled, deep depression spreading through me. I felt baffled and lost, desperately wanting to return with the Sanibels. I was relieved not to be returning to Harvard. I didn't want to spend all my free moments in class. Besides, eventually, they would figure out my skill and experiment on me like that poor Clemmings girl. However, it did piss me off that the Russians took Harvard away from me. Why couldn't the police throw them back in jail? Then, I could live my life the way I wanted to.

I stayed at Peterson's for three weeks. Finally, Child Protective Services said they had found a placement for me. They apologized that it would still take two more weeks to secure it. But they promised I would be very safe and could return to a somewhat normal life.

I found living with the Petersons dreadful. Since I couldn't go anywhere, I sat inside all day. The Petersons would play card and board games with me, but that got dull early on. One could only play so much UNO. When I arrived, they had several stacks of teen books from the library for me. I tried to read a few of them, but they didn't hold my interest for long. They were mushy, and I didn't care for them. I eventually asked if they could pick me up some textbooks. I spent the rest of my time there referencing everything I read. Then, one day, the vibration in my head had returned.

One night, I was awoken by the Russians' energy field. Back at the Sanibels', I had memorized the Russian's energy field as I watched them in the home. Once I knew it, I recognized it. All energy had unique patterns to it, and I realized I knew their pattern. Now, I could feel them outside the Peterson's house.

I could tell they were at the front door. I panicked. I should have used my Zen to reach out to a phone and call 911. But I didn't. I was in a panic, and I couldn't think. I often found when I was full of fear, I had a harder time accessing my Zen. I knew the Russians had a gun, and I needed to get out of there.

Instead of seeking help, I climbed out of the window and ran off, leaving the Petersons to fend for their selves. It was a cowardly thing to do.

——— ◉ ———

I SPENT TWO WEEKS HIDING in the cave, trying to figure out what to do. I was so scared that I couldn't even do experiments. I spent most of the time staring off at nothing. Then, one day, a voice entered my head.

"Why don't you figure out who you are? If you can recall all the maps you have ever seen and retain every scrap of learning material, then why can't you open your mind, review your life, and discover who you are? It is in there just like everything else."

Who did the voice belong to? I didn't know.

I had spent countless hours trying to discover who I was with my logical mind, but I had never tried using my intellectual mind to open up the secrets of my past. If I could solve complex tests, elevate myself to fly, and change matter around with my intellectual mind, I could likely open up lost memories. Could I search the files in my mind and remember who I was?

I went outside and sat on the ground with my legs crossed together. A strong wind blew the smell of damp wood and dirt. A squirrel gnawed on an acorn above me as an owl hotted in the background. The cold air nipped at my arms. I used my Zen to create an energy bubble around me where the wind, smells, and noises could not reach me and distract me. I heated my extremities.

I closed my eyes and switched to my intellectual mind.

I had waited long enough. It was time to open my mind's secret chambers and discover Alora Funk!

Also by Stephanie Daich

Alora Funk
Alora Funk - The Deliverance

Standalone
Out of Breath
Life Chapbook
Phoenix on Fire
World on Fire
Asp

Watch for more at https://stephdaich3.wixsite.com/
phoenix-z-publishing.

About the Author

Stephanie Daich sees life as a gift and opportunity for experience, discovery, and growth. She dabbles in a little bit of everything, including writing. She interacts with the world through the written word and exploration, continuously learning as much as she can cram into a twenty-four-hour period."The most significant commodity is time, and we should never waste it."

Read more at https://stephdaich3.wixsite.com/phoenix-z-publishing.